MW01631526

WISEMEN

The story of three special forces soldiers who agree to a mission to change the world as we know it.

BY
KENNETH BURNETT

simply francis publishing company
North Carolina

Library of Congress Control Number: 2023924366
ISBN: 978-1-63062-056-1 (paperback)
ISBN: 978-1-63062-057-8 (e-book)
Printed in the United States of America
Cover and Interior Design: Christy King Meares

For information about this title or to order books and/or electronic media, contact the publisher:

simply francis publishing company
P.O. Box 329, Wrightsville Beach, NC 28480
www.simplyfrancispublishing.com
simplyfrancispublishing@gmail.com

DEDICATION

To Monta, who showed me how to pray.

Dead Sea, Israel

Table of Contents

Chapter 1 The Mission: Afghanistan Extraction **1**
Chapter 2 Retirement **14**
Chapter 3 Viva Las Vegas **22**
Chapter 4 The Drive for Information **39**
Chapter 5 The Interview **46**
Chapter 6 Details **57**
Chapter 7 Reflection, Thoughts, Decision **62**
Chapter 8 Negotiations **65**
Chapter 9 Making the Right Decision **70**
Chapter 10 Training **74**
Chapter 11 Departure Day **92**
Chapter 12 Passover in Jerusalem **100**
Chapter 13 Getting the Lay of the Land **121**
Chapter 14 Holy Thursday **132**
Chapter 15 Search for the Target **136**
Chapter 16 Dinner and the Mount **139**
Chapter 17 Good Friday - Crucifixion **154**
Chapter 18 Lepros **177**
Chapter 19 Burial and Resurrection **180**
Chapter 20 Preparation for the Big Announcement **191**
Chapter 21 The Return **195**
Chapter 22 Mission Second Half **210**
Chapter 23 Next **213**
Chapter 24 Second Half of the Mission. Continued. **216**
Chapter 25 The Assignments **218**
Acknowledgments **231**

Chapter 1

The Mission: Afghanistan Extraction

I am riding with my team in the tail of a Lockheed C130J Super Hercules transport plane listening to the roar of the four engine turboprop military aircraft, while traveling inside a thunder cloud. We are experiencing the waves of wind as we are hurled right through the heart of this massive storm. These Hercules planes have been well tested since 1954. When you sit in the tail of the plane being bounced around and hearing the plane crack and grind, flying through the worst weather conditions, you briefly wonder just how safe this machine is.

My name is Mark Thomas, Captain of this Recon team, Special Forces, U.S. Army. We engage in reconnaissance and direct-action missions. We sometimes are assigned to peacekeeping missions, search, and rescue, humanitarian, and counter-narcotic missions. Tonight, it's search and rescue and I just so happen to be in charge of the best team anywhere on the planet.

"Hang on tight, men, we are heading into a rough patch," says the pilot over our headsets.

We have waited to execute this mission until now, the month of February, because it is the beginning of the Afghan rainy season. My team operates under the cover of darkness and or extreme weather to successfully complete our missions.

Boom! There's a deafening crash as the plane bucks and bounces. I hear groaning and shifting in the cargo bay.

"Report status," I shouted into my mouthpiece.

"Wahoo!" replies Warrant Officer Paul Jenkins. "This storm has some kick. Did you hear that sizzle? That last lightning bolt knocked out our link to the Eagle's nest."

"How long will it take to restore comms?" I asked.

"Skip, we should pick up the next satellite in about five minutes," said Paul.

"Roger that. Advise as soon as the link is back up."

Paul Jenkins is our tech officer. He is in charge of communications, navigation, and anything having to do with technology. He is as sharp as they come. Just don't ask him to explain what the gizmos do because he will give you a dissertation on electronics and software patches that will last for hours. I trust him with my life. Most of the time I give him a thumbs up and say, "You got this, Paul."

Paul was raised in foster care in Georgia from the time he was born. He went from home to home all over the state until he joined the military when he was eighteen. When Paul was ten years old, there had been a kitchen fire at one of the foster homes. Paul and an older boy tried to extinguish the fire by throwing water on it. This made the fire worse and Paul suffered extensive burns to his right arm. There was no adult supervision at the time and the cause of the fire was never determined. Soon after, Paul was then placed in another home. The fire has always been brought up in our conversations regarding our foster lives. Each time Paul looks down at his right arm and the scar he had received, he becomes really reserved.

When I first met Paul, we instantly became friends. He has

always confided in me. Paul once told me that before the military, he was always searching. I asked him what he was searching for. Paul said he wasn't quite sure but nonetheless, searching.

Paul knew nothing about either of his parents. He said he always thought that there had been a purpose for him, for his existence, but he had not found one except for the military. Paul had prodded tirelessly with the Department of Public Health in Georgia to find out who his parents were, but was unsuccessful. He was so tormented that the Department told him to have an attorney attempt to locate the records. Paul will never give up until he has all the answers he is looking for. I hope for his sake that someday he finds out about his parents.

We nick-named him 'baby brother,' because in basic training he seemed to get picked on quite a bit. I seemed to always be there at the right time, always defending him. You would not know it by looking at him now because no one would mess with this big strong dude. We had to switch his name to 'lil bro' because, not surprisingly, he was getting made fun of for his other nickname.

Paul loves to talk. He once told me, "When I met you, I stopped searching, started to learn, and began living." Paul is always in the weight room when we are not on a mission, pushing his body a little harder each time. I don't understand how a person so fit did not compete in any sports in his youth. Paul's ambition when he leaves the service is to join a rodeo and go on the circuit. He said he could break any horse or steer, and by the looks of Paul, I am sure he could just intimidate the animals into submission.

"Sy, anything to report from the cargo bay?"

"I'm checking now, Skip. That last bolt rocked things pretty good. Be right back to you."

Chief Warrant Officer Simon Rene is our weapons officer. He is responsible for armaments, explosives, and anything involving muscle. As you can imagine, Sy is short for Simon. We did not have too much luck calling him Simon so "Sy" kind of fit and that name stuck.

Sy was placed into foster care in South Carolina when he was three. His momma was white and his daddy black. His parents were not married and Sy believes his Daddy may have left before his momma ever gave birth. This information was based on stories that he heard at the foster homes. He never had any contact with his parents since the day he was dropped off at foster care and says to this day that it is unimportant to ever find out who they might be. Today, Sy stands at 6'2" and is as strong as an Oklahoma bomb shelter, but calm and polite as a church mouse. His heart is the biggest part of his body. Just a big handsome dude who we love. Sy is smooth about putting two sentences together. He can sweet talk a terrorist; but his, "yes-sir, and no sir" are very authoritative.

If you so happen to catch Sy off guard, he may have trouble a bit with his speech, a slight speech impediment, a stutter, that almost cost him his spot with special forces. Paul and I fought tooth-and-nail with our Commanding Officers to keep him in the program and on our team just for that reason. Back Sy in the corner and he will fight. I am proud to call him my friend and teammate.

Sy's ambition is to one day have his own cattle ranch. I had asked Sy if he knew anything about ranching and he replied that he didn't but he sure enjoyed a good steak at any meal. Sy also never took part in any sports activities because he moved around so much. Sy said he was lucky to graduate high school because he had missed so many days. Even though Sy is quiet and seems to always take in so much information, I believe that he may be the smartest and wisest of us all. I say that from my heart because Sy has earned our respect.

Just after midnight, at the heart and intensity of this great weather system moving in, we approached the drop-off point. Our plan is to parachute in with our equipment from the opened rear tail of the plane to a predetermined location. On this mission, we are to retrieve two targets and return with them to our base. Most of our missions are planned during the worse weather conditions and wee hours of the night to give us the best advantage over any opposition we may encounter.

Since the fall of 2020 when U.S. involvement and the occupation of Afghanistan ended, our team has been assigned on numerous occasions, to seek out and extract certain individuals that had been left behind in Afghanistan, for whatever reasons, and return them to the nearest U.S. military base. Of course, we retrieve only people our government deems important enough for the risk we take.

Lately, our missions have been solely here in Afghanistan. The type of training we go through and what type of resistance we would likely expect on the ground or otherwise will vary depending on the importance of our targets. We train for each mission we go on. Depending on how extensive our mission is, determines how much we train. A high intel person would most likely be heavily guarded whereas an ordinary American citizen would probably not. The higher the value of our target, the more extensive our preparations and training will be. My team has had all the extensive training there ever was.

Tonight, I will command this mission with two of the best, the Army has to offer and my best buddies also, Simon "Sy"

Rene and Paul Jenkins. The three of us have been in the service together for just over 10 years and have trained together from boot camp. We eat together, play together, fight together, and most importantly, pray together. All three of us have come from similar backgrounds. We are carbon copies of one another. We each came up through foster care but in different States. We have no parents, at least none that wanted us, no siblings, no family. The three of us just have each other.

How Sy, Paul, and I have been affected in the same way by our foster lives, is remarkable. We each grew up and grew up fast. Those two are my family and I know they feel the same about me. We would lay down our lives for each other and that is a pretty strong bond.

As for me, my life has been almost identical to the other two. I was raised in foster care in Tennessee as far back as I can remember and I have memories of my parents. I was given up when I was about six years old. It seems that the many homes I was placed in always had quite a few kids already housed in them and that each time I moved to a different home I was always the oldest of the group. This is probably where the seed was planted and I obtained my leadership skills. The other kids in the homes always leaned on me for support and guidance.

I was always the skeptical one, I asked a lot of questions. I guess I was lied to a lot in my youth and had a tough time trusting authority. As skeptical as I was, I always doubted the answers I received. I did not get into any trouble so I guess I was the right role model for most of the kids in the homes. I too never got adopted. At eighteen as Paul and Sy did, I joined the service and said goodbye to Tennessee. One thing and only one thing I fear, is leaving the military. I have always had structure in my life and without the military, I wouldn't know what to do and where to go.

Another big thing we had in common, the three of us were exposed to God. Every home that we were each in, made God number one. Every home prayed before meals and prayed at night. Never though, did I realize, that those prayers, and how we learned to pray, would become a significant part of our lives over the next several weeks and beyond.

Our mission tonight is to extract an American couple: locate them and get them out of the country safely. As with most of our extractions, we were given photos and some basic information. The male target, John Doe, had at one time been a university professor before the United States pulled out of Afghanistan. His wife, Jane Doe, is a practicing doctor. Both were under house arrest by the Taliban. A ransom was being negotiated through the CIA. The negotiations had lasted for quite some time because of the fact that our government wanted to drag this out until now and had no intention to pay any ransom. Our government also knew that they were on the schedule to be rescued. The official mantra of the government is 'We do not negotiate with terrorists.'

The weather is horrendous. Thunder, lightning, and wind dominate the scenario. Most of our missions are under cover of storms because of the fact there would be fewer people outside to guard our targets. Tonight, we are expecting very low to medium resistance from the opposition. As we fly closer to our destination, we double-check our parachutes and armament. As the commanding officer of the team, I always create a visual of how I expect the mission will play out and of the outcome, the final result. For whatever reason, I have used this visualization tactic even for small things such as going to meetings, or even the grocery store. I always try to be prepared.

Some call me overly strategically sensitive, but I do not like surprises. I like to be prepared.

We go over some basic time restraints and get ready to go. Tonight, we are dropping a Humvee, a fighting vehicle, that has been modified to provide firepower if needed, about a mile away from our retrieval point to use for our return. The vehicle is equipped with sensors so that we can locate it after we obtain the targets.

"One minute to target, it's a go," and the tailgate ramp opens. We try to push the Humvee out the door but it doesn't move.

"What's wrong?"

"One of the chains got twisted during the storm," yells Sy over the din of the rushing wind.

"If we don't get this baby out of here within the next thirty seconds, we will pass the target zone," says Paul. He starts counting backwards.

Sy fights the wind as he grabs the twisted chain. I see his muscles straining, and sweat glistens on his face. Paul's count is down to five. I prepare to give the order to abort. With a Herculean grunt, Sy yanks the knotted chain. The twisted link snaps. The Humvee rolls free and clears the rear tail door. We breathe a sigh of relief as we watch the parachute open in the night sky.

Within seconds, the three of us are also outside the aircraft, plunging towards Earth at what appears to be a deep dark abyss. As we were heading down, bolts of lightning explode around us. Dropping through the sky is so surreal with the flashes all around and the rain pounding our bodies like big ocean waves. It is like being dropped into a hurricane with the winds exceeding anything imaginable.

We landed on high ground as planned. We secured our snaps and the Humvee. We took cover within range of the target area. We are just outside a small village near Herat, which is the third largest city in Afghanistan. There was no one in sight, no Taliban, no one brave enough to be outside in this torrential rain storm. Water penetrated every open crevice in our uniforms. We sprawled out at our location. The darkness was briefly interrupted by the flashes of lightning. The deluge of rain stopped abruptly as the thunder beat down on the earth and then continued its thrashing.

We have scoped out the area and familiarized ourselves with our target. We leave our place of cover and enter the village. The immense rain caused a flash flood which filled the street around the target area. We spot the target house and move closer. We wade through the waist-high water and maneuver onto the porch. We do not see any lights around or in the house, but we manage to quietly enter the structure.

Once inside, we walked in darkness using night vision goggles, and entered a bedroom. The rain was battering the roof, creating a deafening sound. As we came through the bedroom door, we encounter John Doe who is startled and starts to get up, then Jane Doe woke. I said to them that we were from the U.S. Government and they were to come with us.

"Please, quiet please," I said in a firm but low voice.

They seem willing to accommodate us. Paul was with me in the house and Sy was watching the exterior. The couple grabbed a few things as though they had been prepared for this moment. I handed them rain protection and we began to exit the building. As we were walking out a guard appeared just outside the building and he attempted to get on the porch. Sy quickly silenced him with a single shot from his Sig Sauer P320-

M17 with a suppressor. The guard fell backward, dead. The only sound came when his body splashed into the street.

Reacting to Sy's shooting, Jane Doe froze and seemed to go into shock when we were exiting the front door. I decided that we'd use one of our cloth stretchers and carry her back to the Humvee. Once she was fastened to the stretcher Paul and I carried her through the flooded streets. According to my tracker, the Humvee was a little over three-quarters of a mile away. If we could get through this flooded area, we had an excellent chance of reaching our departure location on time. With the streets and area flooded it would slow down any attempts that the Taliban would make to try and stop us. Any opportunity to gain a few extra minutes of distance between us and our enemies would be beneficial.

Almost as soon as we exited the village and got to high ground, the air raid sirens began to blast. Time was of the essence. We needed to get to the Humvee before the Taliban organized and figured out just where we were headed.

I had thought of the possible positions that the vehicle could have landed; could it be in the trees, water, mud, or right side up? These things go through my head constantly on all these missions and I try to prepare accordingly. I always have a plan A, plan B, and plan C. I constantly evaluate and reevaluate. It's what I do. It rained so hard I was hoping the trek would not be too strenuous on the couple as they appeared to be somewhat fragile. I was also hoping that mud would not factor in too much on this mission at least for us and the next three fourths of a mile. Foot travel and vehicle traction has always been figured into the equation of the missions because of timing. I was mostly concerned about the well-being of our returning targets.

To my hopes and expectations, the vehicle was upright in a field near some trees. It was in what appeared to be the perfect spot. It was not bogged down by mud or any other weather-related hazard. We loaded our targets and our gear and headed north to meet with the chopper.

This was going to be a 5-mile ride, a risky but effective stretch of road, and hopefully an uneventful journey. It is so amazing, the planning and training and factoring in things that may happen during the course of a mission; then trying to complete that perfect mission.

We had prepared for anything that might happen. We prepared for all the glitches and bumps in the road so to speak. Nearing our destination we saw an enemy truck just up the road about a half mile, that had the road blocked in front of us. We saw flashes of gunfire coming from the front and rear of the strategically located vehicle. I knew from our training that when the enemy is shooting so early and from so far away that they probably were inexperienced fighters. Without slowing down and wasting time, we deployed a TOW missile from the top of our Humvee striking the obstructing vehicle and any other interference we encountered ahead. If the Taliban was not sure of our location before, that blast alerted them to our location now. Time became even more important for the successful outcome of this operation.

We arrived at the pickup spot precisely on time. We moved the couple from the Humvee to the awaiting chopper. We loaded our equipment and activated the Humvee that was being left behind, for self-destruction. Our extraction teams never leave any equipment behind that may be used by the enemy to harm us. Before I entered the chopper, and being the last one to board, I turned back and looked all around at the rain, the lightning, and other mayhem that was now starting to brew on the ground, and at that time for whatever reason, I contemplated if this was going to be my last mission.

Our chopper rose as we began our ascent then made a slight turn towards the north. We watched several vehicles driving toward the area where we left the Humvee. Headlights appeared from all directions leading to the field. We saw flashes from the guns that were pointed up and shooting aimlessly toward us and our direction. I believe someone may have entered the Humvee and thought it may have been a gift from the United States because about fifteen seconds after we lifted off the ground, we saw that Humvee explode. Did it ever!

We landed at our base. The Does we extracted on this mission were turned over to some delegates and we were ready to chill for a bit. With steady raindrops still falling, this was a good time for the three of us to have a debriefing on this last mission.

While we were discussing this evening's events, we all looked at each other solemnly. I said to the guys unexpectedly, "Do you boys want to try something different, like civilian life?"

All movement stopped! You could hear things rattling in their heads as they thought for a minute; then they began to ask questions. Paul and Sy had puzzled looks on their faces. We had recently discussed completing our military careers and retiring from the military; not quitting, and going into civilian life.

"Like, what would we do? Where do we go? I don't know man," said Sy.

"This has been our life for so long," said Paul. "But Mark may be on to something. I have always loved the military and what we do but somehow, this is no longer doing it for me. I need more of a purpose, guys, and this may not be cutting it for me anymore either."

"Hold on," I said, "You know we can take an extended leave for a while and if it doesn't work out, we can come back to what we are used to doing."

"A nice vacation."

"Time off."

"We are going back to the States in the morning. When we get to Ft. Carson, we can make the final decision either to take an extended leave or just hang it up. We have the time to talk about it while we are on our way back home. I think it's time, at least for me."

The three of us had never been apart from one another since enlisting in the military. For the next day and a half, we threw out ideas about living the civilian life. We talked about jobs and maybe starting our own business and even pursuing our dreams. We tried to figure out how much we needed to live on. We really had no clue about the cost of living outside of the military.

Slowly, the conversation was shifting from, should we do this to, when we do this. There would be no extended leave for us. We soon convinced ourselves, that this was the time to hang it up. We had been on some tough missions but to leave the military into the unknown was indeed the toughest decision we had to make, so far. Before the military, it was foster care and that is all we knew. We are regimented. None of us had experience with civilian life as adults before joining the military. It was definitely going to be one of the hardest transitions any of us have ever made. But we agreed, it was time.

Chapter 2

Retirement

The morning was chilly but sunny when we boarded another plane, heading home to the States. After our last mission in the torrential rains of Afghanistan, it was time to just sit back a while and not have to be thinking about the next mission or even if there was going to be a next mission. The three of us decided to take a break from our stressful occupations as Special Forces operatives specializing in rescue and extractions. By the time we arrived at Ft. Carson Colorado, we had pretty much determined that we would turn in our papers and get a taste of civilian life.

The first order of business was a debriefing with Brigadier General Fred "Mad Dog" Greer. Paul, Sy, and I took turns using a whiteboard to provide details of the mission. He complimented us on an excellent result in rescuing the professor and his doctor wife from the Taliban.

"Sir, before we conclude, I would like to advise you on behalf of our three-man team, that we will be terminating our service when we complete our scheduled leave."

During the seven years, Greer had been our commanding officer, we never saw him without a cigar in his mouth and a barrage of words on his lips. At my announcement, his mouth opened wide and his cigar fell to the floor. His jaw moved up and down but no words came out. His eyes narrowed as his brain whirred at warp speed considering this news.

After an awkward silence, he muttered, "Erm . . . of course, of course. I'll arrange for you to confer with Colonel Smith before you head out on leave."

We remained standing in the front of the room, waiting. The general was lost in thought. Several minutes passed before he looked up. He looked at us as if he had forgotten we were there.

"Gentlemen, you are dismissed," he said in a tone appropriate for biding a departing lover farewell.

The following morning, we were summoned into headquarters and met with the Commanding Officer and a few underlings. They laid out our track record for the last several years and told us how important we have been and still were to the United States of America. The Commanding Officer reiterated the extent of all our training and that we were the elite of elites, the best of the best.

The three of us were offered large bonuses to stay. We thanked the CO but told him that this too was a team decision to move on. He halfheartedly wished the three of us well and we departed. We shook hands and the Commanding Officer said, "Be careful of your path. You three will be in high demand."

We each were taken into separate rooms where we were loaded up with information on how to transition to civilian life. These counselors that we met with were more helpful by far, than our superiors had been. They explained our benefits as veterans and the Army Reserves Program. I thanked my counselor but had no intention of carrying this military job any further. However, as I was walking out of the office where I had just declined a job, my head was telling me that I may have just made a mistake. That's the way I operate and sometimes it sucks to be me.

Our individual meetings ended at about the same time. We met out in the hallway and high-fived each other and headed to the chow hall to discuss today's meeting. Paul was in his meeting longer than Sy and myself because I know he asked a hundred questions. It was my idea for us to retire but the way the guys were celebrating, I guess I am the only one apprehensive about our decision.

The air was crisp and clean, the smell of a free country! No strings! What beautiful blue skies. Maybe we can get used to this, I thought to myself. Paul and Sy had mentioned a few places that they wanted to see once we were out. I thought that at the beginning we would travel together until we all got our feet wet in this new life. We definitely would always be there for each other. Even if we decided to go our separate ways sometime in the future, we would always have each other to count on.

One of the places that we all had on our list was Las Vegas, Sin City as it was called. We could let our hair down if we had any. We all agreed to travel to Las Vegas. None of us owned a car so I rented a big, white SUV. We would drive to Las Vegas, and then plan our next step once we were there. We were not used to being in a bright white vehicle. Most of the transportation we had driven over the last several years had been camouflaged. We all were a bit worried, myself mostly, that we would stand out. Once we were on the road, it didn't matter, there were more white cars, red cars, yellow cars, and so on; we blended in with the rest of America.

As we jumped on Route 25 South towards Albuquerque, we turned on the music and just stared out the window admiring the mountains and countryside. After a while, we all needed a pit stop so we stopped at a cafe in a town called Springer, New

Mexico. We went inside for burgers and some tacos and of course, a steak for Sy. The restaurant was not too crowded. We liked that, it felt comfortable to us. We talked about tomorrow and the next day and the day after that. We were filled with the joy of exploring this great country that we defended for so long.

I told Paul and Sy that it felt strange not to have to report to anyone, no agenda. Paul smiled and said sarcastically, "Yes, how nice."

We finished our first official civilian meal in the States and we were all pleased.

While at the restaurant, I had this really strange feeling that we were being watched. I didn't say anything to the other two because they were enjoying the experience of being free and eating in this restaurant. Back in the car, I decided to mention what I had felt, my sense, my instinct of being watched, to the boys. They immediately looked around at the other cars.

"You know your instincts are usually right on, but what made you feel that in the restaurant?" Paul said.

"I don't know. Maybe it was just nothing," I said.

I probably should not have said anything because I could tell my two buddies were scoping everything out.

"Guys, maybe I am a little jittery; you know this is all new to us. I really had no reason; the place was pretty much empty. Please don't get excited by what I said."

Paul and Sy quickly dismissed what I said and continued looking out the windows and taking in the sights. They had been in too many hairy situations to disregard a gut feeling. Old Buck, our drill instructor had pounded into our heads, 'The path to survival is eternal vigilance.'

We agreed to stop along the way to Las Vegas and take in some attractions. When we passed a road sign for Flagstaff,

Paul reminded us that the Grand Canyon was nearby.

"Let's do it," said Sy.

We drove toward Flagstaff until sunset. We checked into a motel and went to a restaurant and brewing company. A little road weary, we sat at the bar and ordered a few drinks. We chatted about the military and different highlights of some of our missions ending in strange twists.

"Guys," interrupting their thought process, "I think someone is watching us."

After being spotted, this guy walks over to us, leans into our conversation, and says, "Excuse me boys for overhearing part of your conversation, but by any chance, are you all in the military?"

He seemed friendly enough, I thought, and exclaimed, "Yes we were, how about you?"

Before he could even answer, Paul took the defensive approach and started to ask the guy questions faster than the guy asked us questions. Sy sat back and took a swig from his beer and smiled as he watched this all play out in front of him.

Being older, the man chuckled and put his hands in the air as if he was surrendering and with a sincere smile on his face said "It had been a while since active duty but I still have my connections."

"What the hell does that mean," I thought, "Connections?"

As tensions seemed to dwindle, and walls began to fall ever so slowly, the four of us struck up a friendly conversation. He introduced himself as Jimmy Kish, retired Army. He was wearing a neatly fitted white polo shirt and a sports jacket. He appeared well-groomed and neatly shaven. He appeared military. I usually don't let my guard down but Jimmy seemed very sincere, very likable like we have known him for a long time. Jimmy asked a few questions of us but seemed to already know some of the answers; almost as if they were leading questions. He knew about the military's extraction teams and he also knew about the targets. He knew extensively about Afghanistan which felt comforting because he seemed to be one of us.

We shared a little information about ourselves and that we were recently discharged from the service. I think to myself that I may be giving out too much information. I don't see any danger here if this guy turns out not to be friendly. Besides, who would even think about messing with the three of us?

Jimmy never acted surprised by anything we told him. Jimmy seemed to know the answers before he even asked us the questions. He had asked what branch and how long we were in. I must say this about Jimmy, he did have extensive knowledge of the military. Jimmy was like a counselor, saying all the right things about civilian life and what it's like to make the transition from one to the other.

Our conversation lasted for quite a long time even over dinner that we invited him to. Paul and Sy warmed up to Jimmy quickly. Jimmy was a few years older than us. He carried that professional smile on his face and a trusting look and demeanor. During our conversation with Jimmy, he mentioned a company that may be looking for three recently retired military guys. "If you are thinking about work..."

Jimmy boldly corrected himself, "but, they must be Christians! It's a very religious organization."

He said he knew the pay was excellent and there was no long-term commitment necessary.

"It's a pay-by-the-job kind of deal, not uncommon in the industry."

"I know this because I got a guy . . ." said Jimmy as he laughed uncontrollably. After his laughter settled a bit, he continued talking.

"Seriously, I too work for this company. We are a Research and Development company and we are located just north of Las Vegas."

He said that we should think about employment while we are traveling.

Sy jumped in saying, "Sir, we will need a job in the future, maybe even sooner, what does something like that pay?"

"It pays extremely well! This would be a good first opportunity for you boys. The money you saved up in the military doesn't last forever, you know."

"If you boys would like to go to work give me a call and I can see what I can do for you three."

He gave us his card and told us to have a great time in Las Vegas. Jimmy said he was headed for a business meeting in Henderson Nevada. Jimmy asked for the check.

I said "Thanks, but..." and was immediately cut off by Jimmy.

"Boys, your service has been invaluable to this great country of ours, and this is the least I can do and please accept this small token of my gratitude."

As Jimmy was waiting for the dinner receipt, he turned to us.

"Damn," Jimmy blurted out. "Listen, I just remembered I have this friend who has this suite at the MGM Grand in Vegas. He said I can use it anytime I want for any length of time I wanted. This place does not cost me anything. Let me make the phone call and the place is yours, no strings attached."

Paul and Sy were in full agreement with big smiles on their

faces. I was a little skeptical since we only knew this guy for just a few hours. I thought of one of Old Buck's sayings, "There's always free cheese in a mousetrap."

Watching the expression on his face while he was on the call, it appeared that the transaction was going his way, our way!

"Boys, the place is yours. When you get to Las Vegas check into the MGM, the reservation is under Mark Thomas and the two amigos," he said jokingly, "Again, there are no strings attached, and Thank you for your service."

We could not thank him enough for his generosity. We high-fived and hugged before going our separate ways. Little did we know how extensive this suite was going to be. Vegas was becoming more and more real. With a place to stay, that eliminated one piece of the puzzle. Being in Special Ops, everything needed to be planned. You need to have a plan A and to have a plan B. I plan for success and then think about damage control if things go south. The MGM is plan A, we don't need a plan B, Viva Las Vegas.

Chapter 3

Viva Las Vegas

When the three of us got up in the morning we looked at each other until Paul broke the silence.

"Was that a dream I had or is Jimmy setting us up in Las Vegas?" Paul laughed.

Over breakfast, I asked the guys about our original plan to stop and spend some time at the Grand Canyon.

"I have heard so much about this spectacular place on earth. It is just around the corner so to speak. They say once you are on the rim it is breathtaking; even pictures you see don't do it justice; the colors of the canyon change by the minute as the sun maneuvers across the span of the valley, river, and gorge. They say the hikes down the trails to the river, restore man's respect for nature at its finest. We are so close to this natural, majestic place that we ought to take the time to see and enjoy it."

Sy spoke up to debate me saying, "This offer for a suite in Vegas isn't guaranteed forever; the Grand Canyon will be there forever, meaning, after we leave Vegas."

I could see my suggestion of going to the steep-sided canyon carved by the fast-flowing Colorado River would have to wait. My guys were excited to go to Vegas. They had seen enough of mountains and canyons in Afghanistan and the Middle East and seemed more focused on sitting back and watching dice roll. I didn't blame them one bit for their one-sided thoughts. We, as a group, decided to postpone our stop at the Grand Canyon. We adjusted our plans of visiting one of God's great creations, and headed for Sin City. We all kind of cheered and celebrated our mutual agreement and decided to get the show on the road.

In the recesses of my mind, I couldn't shake the feeling that this was too easy. I kept thinking to myself, 'How did Jimmy know so much about us?' The warning signals were as proclaimed as the call to prayer had been in the middle east when we served. We didn't know what they were saying then and we sure didn't know what Jimmy's intentions were.

I was behind the wheel as the sun's rays draped over the mountains as it slowly rose to take its place in the sky. We would be in Vegas in as little as four hours. Let's go! We did not stop for anything, not even food. The guys were rambunctious, telling each other what they wanted to do first once we arrived. For each road sign we passed, we knew we were getting close. Sy would laugh and rub his hands together like he was collecting some type of jackpot. Paul always talked in depth about the odds of playing blackjack, roulette, and the slot machines.

Sy would be in deep silence, listening to every word Paul had to say about gambling until they were interrupted by another sign indicating the distance to Las Vegas. 'Las Vegas, 175 miles' read one sign. 'Las Vegas, 58 miles' read another. I smiled as the two became more and more thrilled awaiting to begin their adventure. The excitement grew with each mile marker until we reached the golden city.

Freedom felt so good yet I was a bit apprehensive, all of us were. Our lives consisted of foster homes and the military. We had no "civilian adult life, ever." We went from one regimentation to another. Our lives were structured, up until now, and this was a different kind of feeling.

We found the MGM Grand. It stood out so magnificently and sparkly and yes, so Grand. At the front of this monstrosity of a hotel, perched on top of the entryway, is a large bronze sculpture of a lion. When I say large, I mean large like 45 feet tall large! That is probably in honor of Leo, that famous MGM lion that is shown at the beginning of every MGM movie. We had read that the Grand is the largest stand-alone hotel in the United States and it looked every bit of that to us. We were also looking forward to perusing through the six and a half acres consisting of the pool complex, picking out some chairs and just melting for a while.

The MGM looked like a giant diamond perched on top of the earth. There were so many people all over the street, walking and looking. With such a crowd we didn't feel like we were being watched. There were people from every walk of life. We saw three or four people standing in a line snapping their wares on their persons to get the walkers' attention, then passing out some type of card. Some people walking by looked and refused them and others took the card then hurriedly tossed the cards in the air. I can only surmise what's on those cards. They say what goes on in Vegas stays in Vegas. Funny to say, we were now the watchers.

We could not believe that there were that many people who had so much disposable income to come here to Sin City and gamble and entertain themselves. When we pulled up to the valet stand at the Grand, a polite young Hispanic man asked if we were checking in and what was my last name.

"Thomas, Mark Thomas."

"Oh, yes sir Mr. Thomas, welcome to the MGM Grand, I will get you your bags and your guests' bags up to your room right away. Just go through these doors and to your right for check-in."

I thought, wow, what service. Do they give that kind of special treatment to all these people? As we walked into the hotel, the atmosphere grabbed us. Inside the hotel's main lobby was a smaller version of the lion like the one out front. The front desk area was extremely attractive, very modern, with all the colors one could ever imagine. It was also quite busy. People were checking in, checking out and others were just taking in the sights of this grandeur. We heard the sounds of different slot machines, card shufflers, roulette tables, and glasses clinking in the distance.

Hearing those sounds made us want to run into the casino and experience first-hand where the sounds are coming from. Ever since Jimmy had offered this to us, we have, each one of us, been playing winning experiences over and over in our heads, daydreaming our entire stay here. In reality, Vegas wasn't built by winners!

The casinos have mastered the art of creating an ambiance to entice customers to gamble. Their methods are subtle – no clocks, no outside light to alert gamblers to the time of day, and plenty of free booze to reduce inhibitions and clear-thinking. I have also heard rumors that some casinos pump in oxygen to thwart fatigue. This is probably an urban legend. I noticed that the room temperature is slightly above meat-locker level. That will definitely keep you awake. Saturated by the atmosphere in the lobby for a few minutes hooked us with the gambling bug.

Hearing the sounds of the roulette tables and card shufflers, we didn't want to waste any time; we just wanted to go and play.

The three of us were in total awe. We never wanted to leave here, ever.

At check-in, we were greeted by the pretty receptionist whose facial expression changed a bit as she was taken aback when I gave her my name. Without any hesitation, she summoned her supervisor to the counter. Immediately he arrived and welcomed us then presented each of us with a package.

"This is for you Mr. Thomas; This yours Mr. Jenkins, and Mr. Rene, this is for you. Now, allow me to explain," in his British accent.

As he began taking things out of my envelope he said, "These are your show tickets for the next few evenings here at the Grand; these are your breakfast, lunch, and dinner tickets. The restaurant's name is on the front of them. However, feel free to use these at any of the eighteen restaurants here on the property. These accommodations and show times are guaranteed and included in your package. You will not be disappointed with any of these choices of restaurants. Here are your cabana tickets if you feel the need to 'hang about' or just 'laze' by the pools. If you need anything else, please come and see me. We want your stay to be carefree and the best you ever had."

Well, I thought, we really had not been away from our military duties other than a few week-end passes and a week or two fishing when we had furlough so maybe this is what we have been missing. He went on to show us the last item.

"You each have a token to be used for gaming or at any of our shops. You can go to the casino cashier to break this down and to give you smaller denominations."

I glanced at the token and it said $10,000. I thought maybe

I saw it wrong. I took the token and held it in my hand and looked at it again.

I said to the manager, "This can't be right, the meals, the shows, and now this?"

He explained a bit that it was a token of gratitude from, Jimmy Kish, CP Industries. As he appeared to be getting somewhat nervous as he straightened his tie and then said quickly, "If there is anything else you gents need, again, call or stop in at the front desk."

"Oh, by the way, the most important thing," he said with an embarrassed hesitation, "here are your room keys. The lifts, or elevators, sorry gents, are to your left. Enjoy your stay."

We took our packages and keys and headed up to our room and looked at each other in total disbelief. Shocking is the word! The excitement we felt was expressed by us in total dismay and silence as our elevator began its assent. Jimmy Kish had given me his business card and I couldn't wait to call him. I wanted to thank him but I had more questions than gratitude. Why was he doing this and to this extent? Lil Bro and Sy in their minds, were also questioning the contents of the packages.

"That's quite a large sum of money given to us by someone we had just met, don't you think?" Sy said breaking the silence in the elevator.

We were halted from further conversation and thoughts when the doors of the elevator opened. The floor we were on was just stunning. Chandeliers lined down the hallway ceilings and mirrors upon mirrors from floor to ceiling. Flower vases with fresh flowers greeted the guests of each room on that floor. We were on the 45th floor, as high as one could go in this hotel. We located our room and opened the door.

"Holy Shit."

We were in the penthouse with breathtaking views of the city and the Mountains. We had a balcony with a private pool and jacuzzi. We walked around the suite and each found a master bedroom to our liking. We were speechless. Sy started singing and laughing and Paul, Lil Bro, was captivated by the view on the balcony.

I said in disbelief, "Guys, this isn't right, I need to call Jimmy Kish, right now!"

They looked at me like I was taking their favorite food from them. The look they had in their eyes was like, "Don't do it, please."

But we all knew it was the right thing to do, to tell Jimmy we could not accept all this. I went out on the balcony to call Jimmy and Sy rushed out to join me. Sy handed me a card.

"This was on the table next to the champagne and fruit tray."

As I settled into one of the cozy lounge chairs with my phone in hand and Kish's business card in the other, I took the neatly printed card that Sy had handed me and it read,

"Mark, Paul, and Simon, we truly appreciate your service to our country. May God grant you many years to live. For sure He must be knowing, the earth has angels all too few and Heaven is overflowing. May He continue to Bless your lives. Jimmy Kish, CP Industries."

After reading this I felt grateful for what Jimmy had done for us on behalf of his company but I thought it was still way over the top. I needed to share this with Jimmy. It was not a popular call I was about to make but it was necessary. I called the number on the card. I got Jimmy's voicemail. I left him a very thankful message and asked that he could call me back at his earliest convenience.

Sy went back inside.

I stood up and lowered the phone to my side. I was almost numb by what had been transpiring. High on top of this spectacular hotel, I looked out over the city buildings and out onto the mountain range and beyond. I was overcome by a feeling of euphoria. It was as if I was having an out-of-body experience. The rays of the sun were reflecting off the glass windows of the surrounding building and seemed to cast back directly onto me. My eyes were blinded by this glorious light, yet I stood tall. It was the strangest feeling, a feeling like I wasn't myself. I was not able to evaluate and reevaluate. I was only able to experience what had overcome me. The glitter, the glitz; do this do that. What is the trade-off? Moments passed and I felt that I had returned to myself. I can't explain just what had transpired but I knew there was a message there, a message that I needed to understand.

We were all hungry so we decided to go check out the "Buffets."

We scoped out the casino cage to possibly exchange a chip. We decided we would play with our money, the money each of us had brought to Las Vegas. The casino tokens far exceeded anything we had budgeted to spend. If we see Jimmy another time or when we leave this hotel, we will return the three chips.

The evening went well, good food, a great show, and of course plenty of gambling. I didn't get a return call from Jimmy on the first day nor the second day. On the third day I woke earlier than the other two and went downstairs for some coffee and to walk around and get some exercise. As I exited the elevator on the casino floor, I noticed at one of the empty blackjack tables, sitting a little crooked in the chair and half asleep was Jimmy Kish. We both spotted each other at the same time.

"I got your message," he said while shaking my hand with that big smile on his face. "I was in Henderson and thought I would stop to see how you boys were making out. I didn't want to wake you this early so I thought I would wait around till I saw one of you come down the elevator."

I couldn't get a word in edgewise to thank him. He jabbered on about his week and his meeting in Henderson. I interrupted him.

"Jimmy, come upstairs to the penthouse, the other two should be up and we will order breakfast."

"That's a great idea then we can talk and not have so many people around interrupting us."

As we were getting in the elevator, I couldn't thank him enough for all he had done for us, and for his company's hospitality. When we walked into the penthouse, Sy was already up. I asked him to wake up Paul and we would order breakfast.

"Good morning, Sir," Sy said to Jimmy. "We deeply appreciate all you have done for us. It's like a dream come true."

Sy got distracted while talking to Jimmy so I ended up waking Paul, and telling him Jimmy was there. Paul quickly threw on some sweats and darted out to Jimmy.

"Good morning, Jimmy, Sir, we're so thankful for all this. Can you stay for the day and maybe just hang out?"

Jimmy smiled, like he usually does, and said, "I have another meeting today out in the Red Rock area so, I'll only be here for a little while longer. Just checking on you boys. Got everything you need Paul?"

"Sir, more than enough. I cannot thank you enough."

We ordered breakfast and chatted for a while more.

"Boys, I have one more thing for the three of you to consider." I cut Jimmy off handing him the tokens,

"Here Jimmy, we cannot accept these. This hotel and all that this encompasses is more than we ever expected. A hotel room would have been sufficient enough but all this? Thank you again but those things I just gave you, no."

Jimmy took a breath and seemed surprised that I had been so insistent on returning the tokens. Jimmy collected his composure and spoke to us with a more business-like demeanor. But still, inside, we were like kids in the candy store waiting to hear next what he had to say.

"How would you boys like to work for me at CP Industries? I know we talked about it before but this one job came up and it's quite urgent!"

We immediately looked like we were about to ask a whole bunch of questions when we were stopped in our tracks by Jimmy holding up his finger in the air to quell the conversation.

"Let me finish first, this would be a temporary assignment; no more than a month. It is a job I know for a fact that you all do well. 'Extraction.' You boys seem to have done quite well for Uncle Sam maybe we can hire you three for one special mission. You will be extremely pleased with the financial offer. And the most important aspect about this job or as you call it a mission is the spiritual bonus you will receive."

"What's a spiritual bonus?" asked Paul.

"What does it pay?" quipped Sy.

"Well, I can't discuss all the specifics at this time. I, too, have a boss and he likes to lay things out very systematically himself. He will give you all the fine details. Do I think you guys are qualified to do this job? Absolutely! Can you make this kind of money with just one mission? Never! Think about it and if you can't give me an answer right now, I will get back to you later today. I just want you guys to come and meet my boss and listen to what he has to say. We can discuss more about the job then, at another place, like corporate headquarters, the 'Office,' as we refer to it. I asked you a couple of days ago to think about getting a job while you boys were vacationing and that sometime soon you will be looking for work, but this job came up now and I need three brave soldiers. I need three of the best soldiers."

Jimmy wiped his mouth with a napkin and laid it down, he said, "Think hard about coming to work for CP Industries, you will be treated like royalty. Please at least hear more about this one job before you decide yes or no. Go on an interview and talk to my boss. I told him so much about you three and I know he is interested. I will be in touch soon."

Jimmy said goodbye and left.

We barely had time to discuss how we felt about receiving a large amount of money that had been handed to us. We made our point by returning the tokens to Jimmy. Jimmy didn't appear to think twice about it and even dismissed that conversation. I am sure that he got the message, that we couldn't be compromised. He was gone.

As I thought about the tokens, it crossed my mind that maybe we were being tested. Maybe this company is searching for integrity also. I know we passed that test. Maybe just maybe we should listen to what this job may entail. If I am right and that was a test, this may be a company we can work for. This company may be looking for special people, honest and right-mindedness. I expressed my thoughts with Paul and Sy who shared the exact sentiments.

What project, job, or mission is so important that he would want us? What job is so important that they would cater to prospective employees? We've been scouted! We heard some companies hired retired soldiers, and mercenaries to do jobs in and around the world. Maybe this is one of them. Jimmy had a military background.

What is CP Industries? We researched the name and came up with absolutely nothing. We were left hanging in thought. We had a brief back and forth with questions that none of us had the answers to and it became useless to talk about it anymore.

"We know our capabilities and we know what we do best. We have extracted people all over the world and in many dangerous places. That's what we do," I said.

Then Paul said "We should go on the interview and talk some more with Jimmy and his boss. We have more questions than answers at this time so why don't we just go downstairs and chill in the casino? We all have our thoughts. We can sit and think about what questions we need answered when we know what type of mission they want us to perform. We don't even know if it is a mission but Jimmy did say extraction."

We found a blackjack table that accommodated the three of us. Across the table, I half-heartedly asked Paul if he was ready to go back to work?

Sy chimed in, "Hey guys, we just got here, let's just enjoy these next few days, ok?"

All our conversations ended with a question mark. I guess we were curious about what the job was all about. We stayed out the entire night and headed back to the suite as the sun rose. We didn't hear from Jimmy nor did we contact him.

Back in the room we crashed and we were out, asleep, for most of the day. When I got up, I noticed a card under the door. I opened it and it was from Jimmy. 'Call me when you can ASAP.' The boys were still sleeping so I went out to the balcony and made the phone call. Jimmy picked the phone up before the second ring.

"Hey, I am down in the lobby, can I come up for a few minutes?"

Jimmy got to the room quickly and opened the door I had unlocked for him. First thing he said as he entered,

"Good morning, Captain Thomas," he blurted out at 4:30 in the afternoon, "Are you boys still having a good time?"

I considered telling him about our adventures but I could tell he was not concerned about that; it was about the business proposition.

"It's been great," I quipped.

"That's good to hear," Jimmy said. "Listen, my boss wants to meet you three at the office tomorrow and tell you about the job to see if you are interested. He wants to get going on this assignment but wants to give you guys the first crack at it. He is ready to move and I know the financial offer has been significantly increased to make it even more attractive to you three. There are no strings attached, it's a one-and-done deal! I have told him about you three and he is more than eager to talk to you. Let me be honest with you, he is willing to talk about some major financials!"

Thinking to myself, I remembered Old Buck once told me a long time ago, when someone says "Let me be honest with you," does that mean they have been lying to you before? More red flags kept going up but my curiosity was winning that battle.

Jimmy handed me a bottle wrapped in fancy foil paper.

"What's this?"

"A little something extra just for you," he said with a twinkle in his eye. "I know you are from Tennessee and I saw you ordered bourbon the other night and thought you might enjoy it in your room."

I started to unwrap it. Jimmy placed his hand on mine.

"Later."

"Jimmy . . . I don't know what to say."

"I need to run a few errands now but I'll be back at your hotel at seven pm or 1900 hrs. and meet you three for dinner tonight. We can have some more discussion among the four of us. I can sense that you guys want more details about this mission."

Jimmy was a bit forceful. It was the first time he referred to me as Captain Thomas. My thoughts were swirling. He wanted me to be the one to help Paul and Sy adjust their thinking, to persuade the boys to take this job, and to make it work his way. Jimmy had befriended Paul and Sy and they looked up to him, but cautiously. Jimmy was playing head games with the three of us and was probably winning.

When I got to the balcony, I stripped off the paper and gasped. It was a bottle of George Dickel Barrel 17yr Cask Strength Reserve Whiskey. "This stuff goes for several hundred dollars a bottle. Is this guy crazy?"

Paul and Sy got up shortly after Jimmy left and were in pretty good moods after a tough night of gambling and drinking.

"Was that Jimmy that just left?" asked Paul.

"When I got up there was a note under the door so I called him."

"He wants us to work for him soon, like right away: he wants to talk to us more about the job, and he wants us to meet his boss. I don't know. I have so many questions, but Jimmy wants to meet us for dinner tonight at seven."

"Are we in?" Paul said,

"I don't see why not. We have questions, he may have the answers. Let's go."

I noticed Jimmy and Paul seemed to be connecting more. Jimmy knew that I would have the final say and probably thought that if Paul were to put his two cents into the equation it would be the tipping point. Jimmy always said the right things to Sy also, making Sy feel very comfortable. In a short time, Sy never said anything negative about Jimmy or questioned Jimmy's motives. Jimmy knew I would question everything so he worked the playing field around me. I thought to myself, am I making too much of this? Is Jimmy getting in my head too?

"It's a damn job interview! We can take it or leave it. Why am I making a big deal out of this?" I thought to myself.

We freshened up and went downstairs for dinner. We ordered a round of drinks and Jimmy appeared. We said our pleasantries and ordered another round. We ordered dinner and when it arrived Jimmy looked up to all of us and said, "May I?"

With his hands folded, he said, "Heavenly Father, we come to you with thankful hearts. Thank you for bringing us four soldiers together. By your will, guide us to do what is right and just. Lead us, Father, so that we may make you proud. Help us make the right decisions to honor You. We ask for your blessing through Christ our Lord, Amen."

"Jimmy, thank you so much for that," I said, a bit surprised.

Paul and Sy were seemingly more at peace after that prayer from Jimmy. I have not heard Jimmy pray before any of our meals. I am not saying it is a bad thing. What I am saying is, "Why now?" My mind was whirling like a high-powered engine. Maybe I just need to decompress a bit.

"Excuse me," I said to our server, "Can you get me another drink?"

"I don't want to keep repeating myself but you boys will eventually be looking for employment! I have, we have a job that needs to be done soon. Why wouldn't you accept? I will answer that myself. You won't accept the job because you need more details, I understand," said Jimmy, chuckling as he continued.

"No, it's not doing anything illegal; But, just the opposite, it's doing something that's morally right and long overdue. I just cannot get into the crux of the entire operation but I can give you some of the basics. You three will be sent to a specific location; find the person you are looking for, the target, and remove him from the situation he is in, I guess to say, get him out of harm's way. More or less, it's an extraction but in this case, you are just moving the target from one location to another. There is no returning the target to a base; there is no killing the target, it is quite simple. That is something you boys do quite well."

I started to chime in but was cut off again by Jimmy,

"And by the way, it pays really well! Some civilians work years for the kind of money that's going to be offered to you three."

Jimmy persisted.

"Tomorrow morning, I will have a car and driver here to take you to our office. Let us say 0900 hours. It's not too far from here just about forty-five minutes. When you arrive, you will meet with my boss and he will explain the details, all the details. You can make your decision on the spot or take a day to think about it. This, the job or assignment or mission should take no more than three to four days boys, and it pays top dollar."

"One other thing I want to add. There is no long-term commitment. You do the job, get paid, and retire again. This time when you retire you will have a big fat bank account!"

Jimmy kept emphasizing the money. The money, the money, short term.

Paul and Sy chimed in, "Let's drink to that."

"Is that a yes then? Will you come out for an interview?"

I forced a smile. Jimmy looked right past the smile and knew I would be the obstacle in this equation. He knew I would be the one who could end this recruitment for this unknown mission. Jimmy knew that I didn't have enough details at this time and that was causing me to be extremely skeptical of this proposal or job offer.

Why did he say earlier that we needed to be Christians? Why couldn't he share more details? It is obvious that he knows more about the mission. Is this mission top secret? Maybe we need to be in a controlled environment to discuss it further. Why didn't he just say it, if that was the case and why is he being so vague?

Jimmy had Paul and Sy in the palm of his hand, but I was still the leader of this group. CP Industries could probably use just the two but I wouldn't let either go it alone whatever type of mission it was. I bent a little. Not because I wanted to but because I needed to protect my team.

With another forced smile, I said to Jimmy, "We will be ready in the morning."

Chapter 4

The Drive for Information

As I look back, the past couple of days didn't seem quite like a vacation. We seemed to be getting prepped to do a mission that we would normally not feel comfortable doing. The glitz and glitter of Vegas, the meetings with Jimmy, the food, the gambling, and the booze all led us to where we are now. I am eagerly awaiting the one-two punch. I felt in my heart that something wasn't right but just could not put my finger on it. I think that once we will know the extent of this mission, my misgivings will become clear. I hope.

After a long night in the casino, we were awakened by a persistent knocking at the door.

"Go away," yelled Paul as he wrapped his pillow around his head.

"Stop it. We're trying to sleep," I muttered.

"Y'all are impossible," grumbled Sy as he slipped on his luxurious robe and padded toward the door.

"Coming . . . Hold your horses."

Sy opened the door to a server whose smile was much brighter than it had any right to be this early in the morning. A cart covered with gleaming chrome-domed plates, a platter of pastries, and an urn of coffee was at his side. The tantalizing aroma of the coffee wafted into the room. I couldn't help but breathe in the aroma and dream of sipping that first satisfying cup of java.

"You have the wrong room, son."

I almost groaned at the thought of the enticing breakfast being re-routed. But Sy was right, nobody here ordered breakfast. We were too busy licking our wounds from a night of gambling. We had imbibed too much booze to have the presence of mind to order ahead of time.

"This was ordered for you, Sir," the server said.

"By who? None of us placed an order."

"I have no idea, Sir. I just bring it where they tell me. They told me to bring this cart to the penthouse suite. Oh, yeah, here's a note that goes with it."

A note affixed to the coffee urn read, "Be ready for pick up at 0900 hrs. JK."

"Well, how about that? Guys, y'all better get your asses out of bed. Jimmy wants us to be ready by 0900."

I interjected abruptly.

"Jimmy, Jimmy, Jimmy. Do you ever wonder about this guy? He shows up out of nowhere, in Nowheresville, just at the exact time we turn in our papers, then offers us a job that supposedly pays us more money than we could ever imagine. And, on top of that, this. Vegas! How does he know that much about us and what we did, when we never even shared that much information about what we did?"

I hurled the pillow towards the sofa and ran towards Paul's room. "Do you want to see what you're missing out here?"

"Screw that shit, it's too early in the morning and my freakin' head is killin' me. I'm going back to sleep," Paul shouted. "Alright, alright I'm getting up. I am a bit anxious and excited to hear about the extent of this mission. There is way too much intrigue for me just to turn away now."

"Mark, if you want to stay here with Paul that's up to you but the cat is killin' me. I am a free man and free men get to pick and choose what they want to do. If Jimmy is setting the stage, so be it, but I want to see what's behind the curtain."

"That won't be necessary, Paul will be joining us."

Sy's message got through to us and it was rational.

Paul and I collected our thoughts and sat down for a cup of java. We cautiously prepared ourselves for the adventure ahead today.

Dressed and ready, milling around and still taking in the view from the balcony, the phone rang.

Sy who was inside at the time, took the call and said, "OK."

Sy came out to the balcony as we eagerly anticipate what he has to say.

"The car is downstairs."

I had butterflies in my stomach like I always have gotten before each mission. This wasn't a mission . . . yet. It was an interview; we hadn't agreed to anything. But maybe we already did, by accepting these lavish gifts; the hotel, dinners, and other entertainment. Had we backed ourselves into a corner?

I felt a little pressed. I did not have enough information to process this at all. At this moment, I felt unprepared. This was not like me. I could feel we may be getting into a bad situation. I reminded the boys that this was only an interview. Basically, I was reminding myself. I am thinking we can always say no and if I said no how do I convince the other two to agree with me if, in fact, they wanted to go forward? We needed to stay together. Sy was right, it's only an interview and we could always decline the offer.

Paul and Sy were all in at this point feeling totally comfortable with Jimmy. He built them up to a point where Sy and Paul felt they could accomplish anything. Jimmy portrayed them as the finest soldiers that America has ever produced. Building someone up that much, how could they say no to any challenge? My instincts were telling me to get out and get my team out of harm's way, but my curiosity as a soldier said ". . . and tell me more."

Then I remembered what Old Buck used to say, "Curiosity killed the cat."

As we walked out of the hotel, a stretch SUV was parked right in front with doors open wide. An elderly gentleman, apparently the driver, was standing next to the rear passenger door. He sported a crisp uniform with the initials CP embroidered on his left chest. A logo with the two letters intertwined around an abstract design which could have been a cross or an X adorned his hat.

"Captain Thomas, Warrant Officers Jenkins, and Rene?"

He stood ramrod straight and addressed us with such formality that I thought he was going to salute us. Then, he did, snapping off a smart salute. Instinctively, my hand reacted and I started to return the salute before realizing how inappropriate it was. After so many years in the service, I had become used to salutes but it felt uncomfortable seeing this civilian display respect to us retired soldiers. The three of us exchanged quizzical glances as if to say, 'Did you catch that?'

I nodded and we entered the black SUV with dark tinted windows.

"Please sit back and enjoy the ride to the Office. Refreshments and TV are yours for the taking and viewing" as he closed the doors.

"The ride will take approximately fifty-five minutes north and west of here and please if you need anything, or have a question do not hesitate to ask. I am scheduled to have you back here at the Hotel at 1400 hours."

It sort of gave me a little peace of mind knowing we had a return time and that we were not going to be held captive there.

The driver said, "I know they will be serving a lunch there also because our other driver just picked up the caterer."

The ride was pretty quiet. Our conversation with each other was extremely short. We did not ask the driver anything because the questions we had couldn't be answered by him.

The ride started out a bit creepy as we peered out the darkened windows. Las Vegas had yet to come alive. There were a few people with torn and tattered clothing on the street and definitely not your typical tourists. Some people were lying on the sidewalk and appeared to be asleep leading me to believe they might be homeless. Papers were scattered all over the street and sidewalks with work crews in street cleaners, working hurriedly to take in the debris.

As we drove out to the desert, we had to control our expectations. Paul and Sy felt my apprehension and seemed to dial down their excitement. I'm thinking to myself, "Is this crazy civilian life and I left the military for this?"

Sy opened up and amusingly asked, "What type of job you think this is going to be? We have never been in the dark this long about a mission. I will tell you one thing," as he looked out the window, "I sure as hell ain't going into space."

We smirked with a slight chuckle at that comment. Paul added, "You know that Area 51 is out here somewhere. You never know...."

I recalled what the Commanding Officer said as we left Ft Carson, to 'Watch our path.' My head was all over the place as I kept checking the time as we grew closer to the so-called "Office."

Looking out the front window I could see we were getting closer to some type of remote installation, a complex so to speak. It looked more like a base or jail than an office complex. There was nothing around this complex for miles other than desert and hills. It seemed to appear out of nowhere.

As we approached, I noticed that there was a guard house and a gate at the entrance. A fence with razor wire extended around the entire complex area including the several outbuildings that were on the site. This place was huge. We stopped at the checkpoint briefly and without any outside contact noticed that the gate began to roll open. The limo drove past a couple of what looked like newer warehouses, I called them outbuildings because they looked so different than the other structures on the property. They stood out as some type of storage buildings but they were much larger than a barn but a bit smaller than an indoor stadium.

As we continued, we finally stopped in front of an extremely lavishly large office building. Not any office building but a Taj Mahal-type building. The building was all ivory-white marble. The windows that glistened in the sunlight appeared to be cornered in gold. Sy looking out the window, whistled in awe at this huge white elephant seated here in the desert.

"Here we are guys, this is *The Office*," exclaimed the driver in a finalizing, end of the road, statement.

This place was massive. It looked like all the buildings in the complex were connected by walkways or above-ground tunnels. There was an airstrip and a couple of hangers with closed doors. As big as this complex was, there did not seem to be a lot of cars around, actually none other than the one we were traveling in and two twenty passenger Mercedes vans sitting empty and parked outside.

None of these vehicles had any markings on them as you would expect a company to have. Actually, there were no markings on any of the buildings either! No addresses, no company name, no nothing. There was not even an American flag or the State of Nevada flag to be seen. I found it quite strange because Jimmy's business card had "CP Industries" written on it. There was no CP on anything!

I had this freaky thought, *Could CP stand for Communist Party?* I drove this thought from my mind. I kept this radical thought to myself. Things were strange enough already without going off the deep end. Let's just hear what they have to say and not speculate.

The three of us were wearing our best duds for this interview. It consisted of polo shirts and jeans and dress shoes, thanks to Good Will. We wanted to look our best but unbeknownst to us, it would not have mattered anyway. It wasn't our clothes or personality they wanted, it was our skills.

We had arrived as planned and drove right up front to this modern-looking building set in the desert. Towards the rear of the building, we could see covered parking for about 25 vehicles and a heliport on the other side. As we exited the vehicle, I noticed the antennas on the roof and the lighting layout. Paul noticed it also and agreed it was most likely a second helicopter pad on the roof. Also, there appeared to be some sort of missile-detecting device on the roof. I thought to myself this may be a government operation and by the layout of the complex it may even be classified or even a top-secret organization. Paul speculated that this compound would have to cost millions to build at this location and it was definitely a government organization. I muttered under my breath, 'sure, but whose government?'

Chapter 5

The Interview

Our driver hopped out of the car while we were still evaluating the office complex and opened our door. Again, the driver saluted as we exited, and pausing for a moment, uneasily, I saluted back.

As we walked towards the building, the front doors opened and we were greeted by an attractive red-headed receptionist. She smiled and welcomed us each by name and shook our hands as if she had known us for a while. She was wearing a white chiffon V-neck top which not only showed her fine cleavage but also showcased an extremely large cross hanging from her neck. It wasn't fine jewelry and it wasn't costume, it was a hunk of wood that had been plopped around her neck and it looked so out of place you couldn't miss it.

"Come with me to the meeting room please."

We followed her through another set of doors and yet another and into a large conference room. This room appeared darkened at first, yet the light was comforting, very easy on the eyes. The ceiling appeared painted like the sky with moving clouds! This had to be some sort of huge mood room. There was a sweet smell in the air and the temperature was perfect. We noticed how large the chairs were and how comfortable they were when we sat in them. I could see Paul adding up the costs in his head trying to wrap his arms around the number of dollars that went into the construction of all this.

On an enormous overhead screen was a live picture of a Bible apparently from the Bible Museum, Washington D.C. with today's date and current time on the bottom. Toward the top in the upper right-hand corner in bold letters it read, 'JOHN 19:30.' The camera was focused on the passage, dead center:

When He had received the drink, Jesus said,
"It is finished."
With that, he bowed His head and gave up his spirit.

I recalled earlier when we walked through the front doors, there had been this same image on the monitor there also.

We were surprised to see Jimmy Kish walking in from another direction. He was smiling as always.

"Good morning, boys, how was your journey?"

"Great, Jimmy," I replied.

Jimmy shook our hands and slapped us on the shoulders.

"There are refreshments and water and everything you need."

Jimmy always had that comforting smile to go along with his sincere handshake. It put my guys at peace; it made me wonder. Jimmy was definitely a salesman; I wasn't sure just what exactly he was trying to sell us. Jimmy's personality definitely matched the décor of this room, 'I can be anything you want me to be.'

Jimmy stood about 6'1, clean-cut, standing tall, and personable. His clothing was always impeccable. There was never a wrinkle or crease and his clothing fit him perfectly. He definitely had a military background. Jimmy could befriend a grizzly bear or so I thought. He had a unique military tattoo that indicated a cartoon character holding a stick of dynamite. I hadn't noticed it before today because Jimmy had always worn a sports jacket covering his arm, but today he didn't.

We poured some water and mingled a bit until two other men entered the room. Jimmy started to talk to us but was rudely interrupted by a man walking towards us carrying some folders, and speaking with a heavy foreign accent, "Gentlemen, please don't get up, stay seated."

As he walked towards the head chair in the room, Jimmy looked perturbed but took a seat with us. Walking just a little distance caused his breathing to be labored. He was short and stocky and very much overweight. If he was the big guy, his clothes were a disgrace. He wore a dirty open-neck shirt, soiled pants, and had dandruff on the lapel of his jacket. The clothes were definitely high end but I thought you might have to clean them now and then.

"Excuse the unpleasantries and let's get down to business. My name is Jake Lepros," he said breathing heavily.

I could see the veins in his neck were sticking out and the redness in his face deepened as he spoke to us. He did not look up at us; he did not look us in the eyes. Lepros and I locked eyes for one moment and for that one instant, I saw daggers. Lepros continued to avoid eye contact with us while he spoke.

To me, this guy seemed totally agitated, angry. I sat there thinking, 'This guy wants us to work for him and he is talking to us like this? What a piss-poor presentation of himself.'

"I am the owner, CEO, Chief financer, and so on of this operation. I started CP Industries many years ago. I have investors from all over the world seeking what I have now created, and they, through their generous infusions of cash, want to be a part of this endeavor. We are close to completing this very special project, which took several years to develop. It was always an aspirational thought but once we had created artificial intelligence, this project moved with great speed to reality. We learned and developed what we needed, quickly. We are not a government agency or affiliate."

"CP Stands for 'Christ Project.'"

The three of us looked at each other in amazement and our attention grew even deeper. Lepros had years written all over his face. The lines on his face were not age lines but I saw them as terror lines. Maybe I was a little too judgmental with what he had just conveyed to us, but it surprised me when he said the Christ Project when he looked like the devil, pure evil! I had an instant feeling that I did not like this guy at all. Being a Christian man, I should not judge someone by his appearance or mannerisms. We were here and I needed to give my full attention, without prejudice, at least that is what I should do.

Lepros went on to speak with an authoritative voice.

"We looked at many, many candidates who we thought could pull off this mission. We researched yours and others' backgrounds and military records. You have been personally selected by me to be my soldiers, mercenaries, and would have one job or assignment as you might call it. Gentlemen, I don't like the name mercenaries so let's say the positions call for 'Soldiers of Christ.' That is how we will refer to you as, Soldiers of Christ. You are asking yourselves why Soldiers of Christ?

Let me backtrack just a little and tell you about the mission. As I said earlier, since the inception and development of artificial intelligence, we have made tremendous strides towards planning and formulating this mission."

I am daydreaming ahead of anticipating just exactly what this guy has to say and the words 'Artificial Intelligence' is sticking in my brain. My first thought is that AI would be a plus and to our advantage for whatever the mission may be.

I looked over at Jimmy and he was uncharacteristically stone-faced. He doesn't look like he is excited to hear more. He seems to be more interested in seeing our reaction when the mission is unveiled. Paul and Sy are sitting on the edge of their chairs and eagerly awaiting the goal of the mission.

"Gentlemen, one of the most hideous acts by mankind ever committed, was the trial and conviction, the torture and killing of Jesus Christ. All agreed? It was so atrocious that even after over two thousand years people are still talking about it. Man has never, ever seen that type of torture on anyone let alone our Lord and Savior. At the time of his torture and Crucifixion, not one, not one other person around him, not even his disciples, lifted a hand to try to save the King of the Jews, their King, from the Cross. Maybe they feared reprisals from the Roman Guards. Maybe they were in shock. Maybe they were cowards. Regardless, no one stepped up to defend Jesus."

We nodded, highly focused now on what this man was about to say. Each of us searched our own minds putting ourselves in their positions and trying to fathom how we would have reacted. Lepros broke the mood of introspection.

"If someone, at that time, would have just come forward and rescued Jesus, saved him from that brutal death, life would be so much more different than it is today. Christianity would be flourishing instead of declining. Sadly, out of all his followers and believers, no one dared to step in and save him from that mess that He endured. I have thought about this so many times for years. It is heart-wrenching. I have dedicated my life to figuring out how to remedy this. I vowed to develop the capabilities to do something to save Jesus. I now have those capabilities! But I am an old man, I could not possibly do it, alone...that is until now."

Whoa, ears up, good buddy, here it comes! There was no daydreaming now, the cat is almost out of the bag.

"Gentlemen, with your assistance, a small army of three, we can save Jesus and save Christianity. You three are the perfect fit. I know you have heard of artificial intelligence, have you not?"

We nodded but still wanted more information. Sy was just about standing edging closer and closer to being totally separated from his chair. I'm not sure we do understand AI but we are mesmerized by Lepros. It's almost like we have surrendered our free will. He is appealing to our professional pride and our strong religious beliefs.

"Think about it gentlemen, no one defended the greatest person that ever walked the earth. Now on the other hand, if we could wave a magic wand and save this man, Our Lord, from this atrocity, just think of all the miracles he would still have been able to perform. God would again put him in a position to show the world that He is our King. Do you agree with what I am saying?"

Lepros for the first time, stared at each one of us.

I am thinking, where is he going with this? We all smirked at the term magic wand.

Lepros, in an authoritative and demanding voice, shouted: "How much do you love Jesus Christ, our Lord, and Savior? What I am saying to you, gentlemen, if Jesus were to live and not die on that cross, we could save Christianity!"

I thought to myself, "Did he say we? This is starting to sink in but..."

"I do not want to bore you with the technicalities however,

we have developed a device that can send people back in time, anytime, even to the time of Jesus, where he could be saved, extracted as you would call it."

He paused, surveying the room to gauge our reactions.

I still didn't get the gist of the matter. It didn't sink in. I am still a bit lost trying to digest what Lepros is saying; back in time; save Jesus. I could see Paul and Sy mumbling to each other with confused looks on their faces. Jimmy has his head looking down towards the table at a closed folder where he is seated seemingly trying to hide and the guy next to Lepros, hunched over the table, had a pen in his hand that he keeps wiggling back and forth waiting to put his two cents into all this. Lepros never introduced this guy seated to his right but occasionally Lepros leans toward him and shares a brief conversation.

"Gentlemen, you three could be the ones to Save the Son of God!" It just set in! Paul stood up holding his head in disbelief. Sy dropped his head just over the table. Me, well, I'm trying to take all this in and the reactions of my team.

"A time machine? You can't be serious," I roared.

"Christianity would be saved and have a new meaning. Love would be all around us, and wars, there would be no more wars, no hunger, no poverty. You three can save the greatest person who ever walked the earth from Crucifixion. Jesus needs to only be freed from that vicious killing. Once he is free from harm, from that Crucifixion, your job would be complete. You will return here, home. Jesus will not return with you which makes your mission that much simpler. Jesus will just need to be freed from the Crucifixion, with your help. He would be freed, free to reign as our King."

"Are we talking a time machine?" I blurted out, still

dumbfounded.

Paul and Sy are now staring at each other.

"Gentlemen, this may sound extreme, unreal, unbelievable, but what I am asking you is this, we would like to send you back, you, your team, back to the time of Jesus, and you, you save Jesus from the cross. You save Christianity! We now have the capability to do just this. What we need now is a team that has experience and can easily be trained to fight if needed the Roman and Jewish soldiers. I need a team who can go and save Jesus: I need a team that can save Christianity.

"If God and Jesus have been the cornerstone of your life like they have been in mine, you should consider this proposition."

Lepros leaned toward the guy to his right, whispered something, and got an acknowledgment.

"We need more information about this time machine."

Paul and Sy nodded in the affirmative.

"Our computer, our time stamp machine, as I call it has been thoroughly tested. It works extremely well. We have this time machine; all we need is you three. We have tested this time machine and have sent other people back in time and they have returned unscathed. We know what it's like there, in Jerusalem, at that time. We have been there. What we need now, are professionals, experienced soldiers, to travel back and save Jesus Christ."

"How long does this mission take?" Sy interjected.

"How long has this time stamp machine been around?" shouted Paul.

"We only need about a week and a half to complete this entire mission. The actual mission should take roughly about three or four days tops. We are looking at about a week for training and planning. This is your chance; gentlemen. God our

Father is your guide. He will protect you and you will one day be handed the keys to heaven. You go, you save Christianity. Not only do you save Christianity, but you will also be paid handsomely in return."

Our jaws dropped! Time machine! We have never in our career, been briefed on a mission that we couldn't successfully accomplish. This mission is different. How is this possible? Are we guinea pigs or something? I need more information! A lot more information.

"I know you are shocked by this but I assure you through all our testing, that our equipment works flawlessly and it is completely safe," bellowed Lepros.

He paused, we stared at each other and we were still stunned when Lepros said again, veins puffing and face becoming redder, "Gentlemen, gentlemen, for the love of Almighty God, for the love of Jesus, and the rewards that you will reap, not only here but in heaven, eternal rewards, consider this mission."

I could see Paul, now walking in small circles, occasionally bringing his hand to his head, trying to digest these last few minutes. I could see the anguish on his face. He was fighting himself internally.

Sy gained his composure and sat tall. He asked Lepros about the pay.

"Now for the icing on the cake and your earthly reward, if you accept the mission, you will each be paid five million dollars. Half of that money will be deposited in your accounts before you leave."

Lepros again nodded to the guy to his right who now looks into the folder he is holding. My speculation is that he, the guy to his right, is the money man.

"You will receive the other half after the mission has been completed and you return."

"When would you want us to perform this, Mission?"

Without waiting for a reply, I said nervously, "Right away, next week, next month?"

"Gentlemen, this money should last you a lifetime. However, money should be the least important factor in your decision. And the answer to your question Captain, NOW!"

In a creepy turn, speaking very slowly, saliva now dripping over his lower lip, and softly Lepros said, "How much do you love Our Lord and Savior?"

When Lepros spoke to us I got mixed feelings, that deep down something wasn't right. We either were not being told the whole story or, he was genuine and his heart and soul were in it and that it was up to us and only us to save Jesus. From appearances, Lepros did not seem like a God-fearing, God-loving person but again I was getting mixed signals. I guess looks could be deceiving.

What he appeared and presented himself to me, was a demanding old man, set in his ways with a very dark personality. Lepros appeared to me as one of the darkest people I have ever encountered. I was wondering if he had a hidden agenda. I was maybe a little overly judgmental at this time in my life; but then again, maybe not. What he was asking of us would be to perform the greatest mission, the greatest feat ever accomplished by any one team, ever!

"My friend Sid Green will be addressing us shortly, oh here he is now. Sid will give you the details of the mission and how it works. Sid will also answer the technical questions you may have. Gentlemen, I would like an answer today, if you will accept or not. I would like to get this mission started right away as soon as possible so please keep in mind all I have offered you in return for your commitment to this mission."

"Gentlemen, I need to excuse myself and turn it over to Sid"

Lepros got up and quickly exited the room before we could ask him any more questions.

Sid appeared to me as a cross between a computer geek and a want-a-be military guy. Sid was very thin, and short, with glasses. He wore a dark military kakis jumpsuit; definitely looked like a hands-on guy.

Lepros seemed so nonchalant about the actual time machine part of the mission. He was like, 'Hey guys, go back in time, do your thing, and come back!'

Chapter 6

Details

Holy shit, . . . literally! This guy wants us to travel back in time, save Jesus from Crucifixion, come back home, get paid, then go about life as if nothing happened.

"Good morning, gentlemen," said Sid who nodded at me, ". . . Captain."

"I cannot say let me be brief because I know you have a thousand or two questions. First and foremost, this is a highly classified mission. I want to tell you that getting you there to the time of Jesus and the Crucifixion and back here, is the easy part of this mission. You guys doing what you do and do best is the part where we here have no control. If I was capable and could have gone back or Mr. Lepros could go back and save Jesus from the cross, we would have done it already.

"But we need soldiers, trained soldiers, a small team who works well together and who gets missions completed. That's why you three have been chosen; of course, chosen to interview, you three will ultimately make the final decision whether you accept the job or not. So, if you are comfortable with, and when you get comfortable with what, we do, and we are comfortable with what you do then the mission should be a no-brainer, correct?" Sid was not waiting for a reply.

Sid spoke in a calm, matter-of-fact but nervous voice. He stood as he spoke to us. I assumed because of his height, we would tower over him, making him more nervous than he already was. Sid tried his darndest to make everything appear smooth but the constant pushing of his eyeglasses to his head as he was talking to us was a noticeable distraction. We were trying to figure out the mission and size Sid up at the same time.

We asked several questions and none of them were about money. We asked about the time stamp, the time machine that will whisk us off. Sid explained, "The details would be covered in training, but basically you would enter a chamber much like an MRI machine. Every cell in your body would be scanned, copied, and uploaded into a computer file. The logistics would be downloaded also into a separate file." He paused. "Along with the logistics, we are able to merge another file, languages. Our computer takes all three files and puts them together. For instance, we would load Hebrew, Aramaic, and Galilean into the files. When you arrive in the year of Our Lord, you will be able to understand and converse in those specified languages."

This is an awful lot to absorb right now I thought.

"Logistics would also include the dates of the events and the longitude and latitude of each location. These two files will be merged through artificial intelligence, and be reconstituted at that location, specifically Jerusalem in the year of Our Lord's Crucifixion. Your bodies, would be recomposed much like a 3-D printer. Your copied cells would be merged with the logistics and printed out in a separate file, the past. To give you a simpler description, with the aid of the body chamber, it allows your bodies and cells to be 'sucked' into the past and placed at the designated location. On the return, it works in reverse."

Sy and Paul both stared at Sid, speechless.

"With this sophisticated device, we can program the coordinates destination, then program the time of arrival. The return part is even easier, we handle everything at this end at a predetermined time, unless," hesitation by Sid, "there is some sort of need to be transferred back sooner. An example would be if the mission was accomplished sooner than anticipated."

"Mr. Lepros has told you that this has been performed successfully, correct? I was the one that has gone back in time. I have been to Jerusalem at the same time you boys will be going back. I have seen Jesus Christ!"

Sid nervously adjusted his glasses.

With that being said, slowly I could see each one, Paul and Sy, leaning toward accepting the mission. It was like the switch was turned on. My boys were in hook line and sinker but why wasn't I as convinced as they were? Why didn't I feel I needed to jump into this the way Paul and Sy felt?

We talked for a good two hours more with Sid. Many questions were asked about the time travel. What does it feel like and how long does it take to get where we are going? How do we know what Jesus looks like to save him?

Sid had some brief answers but led us to believe that some of the questions would be answered in training since we hadn't officially accepted the job. He did assure us that the time travel part of this mission was safe. Jimmy stayed also but remained unnaturally quiet but listened intently. We also asked Sid about his travel back in time. We asked if there was documentation on his travel.

"All I can tell you now is that each one of my trips back in time was successful, with no issues at all. Every mission is classified and I have documentation. The transcripts of our missions could be provided to you."

"Trips? Like multiple?"

Sid never responded and was interrupted. A staff member

entered the room and advised Sid that lunch was ready. Before the meal was brought in, Sid stated that Mr. Lepros, needed a decision today or at least by morning. Sid said that if we couldn't commit to this mission right now that we should sleep on it and pray about it.

"But I urge you three, right here, right now, to accept this mission. God will lead you to the right decision I am sure," Sid added.

I chimed in and being the forceful leader that I am said, "We can't make a decision like this, for a mission of this nature, in 24 hours, Sid. You have asked us to do something no one has even heard of doing before. Time machine, Jesus, Crucifixion, to say the least, and exactly, what are the religious implications? This sounds so far beyond our pay grade; I am almost speechless."

Paul and Sy looked a little disappointed but relieved that I had taken an authoritative position on this mission. They sensed that I was in total control not only of the decision to be made whether we accept the mission or not, but of their safety, too. I had always had their backs on every mission and they both knew it. I did not waver one bit when our safety was front and center.

Even though I was a bit apprehensive about this mission, I was still intrigued by it. The thought of being face-to-face with Jesus and diverting the Crucifixion to save his life was overwhelming. I wanted to give Sid a chance to sell us on this mission. I did not want to say "Yes," without more data.

"Sid, come by the hotel this evening and be prepared to answer all and any questions we have." I knew this would give the three of us time to think about what we are being asked to do and to come up with more questions. I told Sid that it will not be a short stay for him because we had never crossed this realm before. Sid agreed and Jimmy who had been silent during the entire meeting said that Sid and he would come by this evening.

Lunch was served but I was not even hungry. The anticipation did not fade but grew tenfold. It would be so easy just to say, 'get somebody else' but that is not how this team operated. Besides, I didn't want them to get anybody else.

This was just not a mission anymore, this was our souls and eternity, and doing the right thing, the thing that God wants us to do. We needed to make the right decision.

Sid said that he would gather some information that we may find useful and bring it to the hotel this evening and that we should expect him about an hour after we arrived. We left the 'Office' compound and were still stunned at what we just heard.

After lunch and right on time, we were escorted to the reception area of the "Office" where our driver waited for us. I looked again at the overhead screen as we were walking out; Todays date and time, current; JOHN 19:30. We reseated ourselves back in the stretch SUV and Jimmy asked to join us on the ride back to our hotel.

Chapter 7

Reflection, Thoughts, Decision

Jimmy knew much more than he had let on. He was holding back the whole time. Jimmy wasn't his smiley self and remained somewhat quiet the entire ride back to the hotel. He apologized for the gruffness of his boss but added that, "Lepros means well. Most of the time he does not leave the complex and works sometimes around the clock. He is all in on this mission and the importance of it."

That explained his clothing I thought to myself.

When the time is right, I will ask Jimmy, when were we in the crosshairs for this mission?

They knew how capable we were of pulling this off if we accepted the mission. I guess the recruitment part isn't that important at this point, the important thing is, do we accept?

Jimmy broke the silence and reminded us that what was said at the meeting "is indeed, highly classified; the mission, the expected travel, and other details."

"Y'all have top secret clearance so it's no different than any other mission you boys have been on. I could not share too much with you earlier because I didn't know exactly what the mission was about until you guys did."

I believe that Jimmy was with us now here in the limo, for one reason and one reason only; to monitor our behavior and report back to Lepros.

“Let me say this, you may have even been told too much because you haven’t accepted the job yet. But, in all fairness, since this mission is a little exceptional, information had to be given to you about the time stamp and time travel.”

When he said that Jimmy reached back and scratched his head in an awkward manner. Paul noticed it also and gave me a look. I looked at that slight motion as a possible sign of deception. We traveled the rest of the way back to the hotel in utter silence.

* * *

Back at the Office, Sid and Lepros met in closed quarters. Lepros was feeling miserably angry because the three of them didn’t accept the mission right away and yelled out to Sid,

“I don’t care what you have to do, those three will do the mission! Get a commitment today! If they try to back out call the exterminators and make them disappear in the desert. Sid, I don’t care what the hell you have to tell these guys, but I want them on board, now! Promise them anything you have to, to get them onboard for this mission. I put my all into this and I don’t like failure.”

Lepros let out a laugh looking at the overhead monitor, “One day soon that saying will no longer be there. We are so close. It will no longer have any relevance. Sid, put together data sheets from time travels and only share them if they are mentioned this evening. I want those three on board now! Today! I have worked my whole life to make this planet my Kingdom. We are so close now I can taste it. The Jew needs to be kept from the cross. Erased from history!

“Sid, I make a living off the greed in people’s hearts. That is how I am able to buy them, pure greed. Everyone has a price. I put my useful idiots in positions of authority to work for me!

They are useful idiots that I control!" laughter from both.

"You promise them anything, you hear me? These three, the three stooges, will be part of my most successful project yet."

Lepros looking at Sid said, "Get them to accept, and you know the rest of the story."

Sid grabbed some literature that had been recently printed that asked the public, Christians, to donate to the Christ Project. So much money had poured in for the advertised Christ Project but no one knew what it was for, but they donated anyway. Lepros started this phony company to finance this mission; the mission to save Jesus. What it did was take more money away from people so that Lepros could use it to buy other people for his own evil doing.

Chapter 8

Negotiations

Sid arrived at the hotel on time and went up to the penthouse. The boys were all congregated on the balcony.

"I know you have so many questions but I need to get one thing out of the way. I told you I have been personally sent back in time!"

That was a show-stopper and a conversation starter! That was the one statement we were all intrigued about and wanted to know more. We all froze but Jimmy, who was looking for some ice. We didn't see what was coming next.

Sid opened up to us. "I went back to 1865, April 15, to the Peterson House. President Abraham Lincoln was shot the evening before. I watched him die in that house."

There was a long pause from Sid. Silence from us.

"I also went back to 1953, June 2, at Westminster Abby in London to view the coronation of Queen Elizabeth II. I was at both places, perfectly placed, and was returned at the exact planned time.

"I have done it. On three occasions nonetheless. Then, the most recent, I went back to Jerusalem and saw Jesus! I was just one man there. I couldn't save him. I saw the guards, the city, the disciples, and Jesus, but I knew I couldn't get him out. I could not do anything but report back. I had no equipment, and no skills for that type of operation. I felt helpless."

"What did he look like? How did you know it was him? Did you see him get crucified?" My goodness, Sid, don't leave us hanging.

"Guys, I need to be perfectly honest with you, I am already telling you too much information. Each mission is classified and if the government knew of our capabilities, they would shut us down. This is a highly top-secret operation. You boys have yet to accept so I can't divulge too much more information."

Sid's phone rang, "Excuse me."

After a brief conversation, Sid went on to explain how the time stamp works.

"In our world here and now we use latitude and longitude to locate certain places on our planet. There is an identical formula for time also. If an event occurs, it has happened. The starting point is always right at this moment. The here, the now, is always zero!

"We have mastered going back but we can't go forward into the future because nothing has happened going forward yet, to apply it to a formula. We can't go forward to measure an incident that hasn't yet happened. That is why with the time stamp we can only create a formula for events that have already occurred. Hence the past. Events in the future cannot be programmed because they have not happened. There are no measurements for going forward, yet. At least not on this parallel. If that makes any sense."

"So, you are saying there is no time travel to the future?"

"That's correct, because nothing has transpired that there would be a record of that event, measurements, understood? Through artificial intelligence, we can put in a place and a date and even a time and arrive there within five minutes of the actual programmed time. Why is it not exact, well we are still working on that but that piece of the puzzle is relatively minor. When you walk onto what we call the space-time placement platform, all systems are activated. You feel like you're in a state of euphoria. Almost instantly, you are at your preplanned, preprogrammed location. I take this was the part you were concerned about, correct?"

"How precise is the location? What happens if we are transported into the middle of the Roman barracks?"

"You boys aren't afraid of a few Roman Guards, are you?"

A little dry uncomfortable laughter followed.

Although Sid turned the question into a joke, I noticed that he never answered it. I'm concerned that he is dancing around serious issues. Playing Devil's Advocate, maybe he can't reveal too much because we haven't committed. Yet, how can we commit without answers to serious questions? I recall Old Buck saying that if a soldier thought about every order, he would end up paralyzed. One of his mantras was 'Leave the thinking to the brass and just follow orders.' He said that he adapted this from the famous poem *The Charge of the Light Brigade.* I don't worry about that but it was a maxim that had served us well in our careers in Special Forces. Too much thinking could get you killed.

Sid went on, "There will be about a week or so of training, a simulator, weapons, culture, and so on. You fellas would be sent out and returned in approximately three days. By the way, this will be the longest mission yet. I was only gone for two days."

Sid nervously adjusts his glasses. Although his fidgeting made me suspicious, the other guys seemed unaffected. They were listening attentively, looking at Sid as if he were Moses coming down from Mount Sinai.

"There are some logistics we need to go over in training and we will review the Bible as it attempts to give us some locations that Jesus should be at during certain days.

"Captain, this is where your team comes into play. We need to avert the Crucifixion. We need to get Jesus out of that situation sometime while he is in Jerusalem. We need to save him from the cross before the specific time of death in order to save Christianity. It will be at a certain point in that final week when it would be the easiest to get him out of there. Yes, you will meet Jesus himself, face-to-face. There will be no need to kidnap him just to free him and send him away, help him escape. On Good Friday, the Friday we now celebrate, we will bring you three home, at 1500 hrs. That will give you the entire time, three days to effectuate the saving of Jesus."

We talked until 03:30 hours and felt more comfortable with the answers we had been given about the mission so far. Lepros knew it was a go because of the eavesdropping devices he had secretly planted in the penthouse. He listened to the entire conversation and texted and called Sid when he wanted to interject something into the conversation.

We just assumed Sid was a busy man because he was always on his phone. Sid was in his fifties and said he had been with Lepros for about thirty years. They seemed comfortable with each other. Sid was an extension of Lepros, a kinder, gentler extension. "Sid, one more thing, what's with the monitors at the office? John 19:30?"

"Captain, we will discuss that once we receive an answer from you and your team."

We kept our instincts about Lepros to ourselves but I guess he heard them anyway after Sid left.

Jimmy was a little edgy and said, "Well, boys, what do you think? Think you can pull this off? Are you interested?"

"Of course, we are interested Jimmy," I said. "We wouldn't have invested this much time if we weren't."

"Is that a yes then, Captain?"

"Let me talk with boys in private and I will give you an answer in a few hours."

Jimmy stayed and had a few beers with the boys, I went to sleep. I needed to reach deep with this one. I asked myself, "What if there is a malfunction with the time stamp? What if we are killed during the transport to or from? These are the same questions we could have had when we were being transported to our missions in the military but we didn't. Aircraft are normal operating procedures. They were not at one point in history just like this time machine. Are we afraid of this machine that we don't know anything about, or are we afraid of the mission? We could easily complete this mission successfully now or in the past so it must be the time machine we are worried about. Or maybe, it's us being in the presence of Jesus Christ!

Chapter 9

Making the Right Decision

I got up early the next day and used my phone to find a church in the area. I dressed and went downstairs and grabbed a cab. After giving the driver the address, I asked him to wait while I ran in.

I found an empty area and sat down. This is who I needed to talk to. This is who I needed for advice. He had always given me the right answers to my questions and answered all my prayers. I was not alone.

The church's interior was very solemn, and peaceful.

I bowed my head and said softly, "Father, if this is what you want me to do, so be it. You have protected me my entire life. I can do this if this is your will."

At that exact moment, a breeze grabbed the front door pushing it open ever so slightly. The light rays that entered the opening of the stained-glass door were magnified and refracted across the other stained-glass windows causing my vision to see a spectacular circular rainbow of colors around the altar.

As the wind died down, the door closed and the brilliant light subsided. I knew then that this was the sign. God wanted me to go forward. I left the church noticing the still air in the Vegas Valley. The cab was waiting and the driver took me back to the Hotel. The boys were still in their rooms.

"It's time to go to work," I yelled out knowing that at any

moment I would get a reaction from them. Their doors opened and one by one they came out onto the balcony.

I talked to Paul and Sy when they sat down,

"The three of us have talked about this assignment. There is no fear factor in doing the extraction. Our transportation, the time machine, to and from the mission is what I believe we were having trouble with. We have taken chances before, even unknown risks. This is what we are and what we do. I say let's do it!"

Paul and Sy rose up from their seats with genuine smiles on their faces and hugged and high-fived each other. I knew them not only as soldiers and friends but as Christians. If this is what God had in mind for us so be it. If God has other plans, so be that too.

Before even telling the boys, what had happened earlier this morning, in church, I had called Sid and told him that we would do the job and to tell us what the next step was. Sid had already known we were going to be up for the assignment but was reassured once he heard my tone.

"Let me inform Mr. Lepros of your decision and I will get back to you."

While we were downstairs in the hotel restaurant having a more or less celebratory breakfast, the phone rang. It was Sid.

"Congratulations on accepting the mission, Captain. Tomorrow at 0700 hrs. come downstairs. The car will be waiting to bring you three to the Office where we will begin to prepare for the mission. We would like to send your team back in time, to Jerusalem, in about a week. That should be plenty of time for prepping and training."

"What about the hotel and our rental car?"

"You will be gone for a few days then back in Vegas soon

after. You guys can check out anytime you want, or stay as long as you like."

That was reassuring that Sid was so sure we would return from this mission. We started to plan our evening's events when I hung up the phone. While Sid was with us in the wee hours of the morning, he had given each one of us our tokens back and added, "with no obligation," and left them on the counter. Now, this morning, we each had our $10,000 token on us and decided that this was our partial down payment for our upcoming job. We got up from breakfast and headed to the casino.

Little did I know, or even cared to know that Sid was and had been sitting with Lepros when he called me.

"They are in," exclaimed Sid.

"Now let's celebrate!"

We had a day to try and unwind a bit here with so much off our plates, at least this part anyway. Sy got up first, grabbed a coffee, and went to the blackjack tables. I followed and we chatted for a bit about the recent call we had with Sid.

Paul came out of the gift shop with a great big pair of sunglasses exclaiming, "Damn it's bright out here."

"We start work tomorrow!" I said to him and Sy in somewhat disbelief. "0700hrs we will get picked up to start training. We should be back, in our hotel, mission completed in about a week and a half."

"Let's have some fun today and call it quits early," shouted Paul with a big smile on his face. "I would like to be well rested for our first day on the job."

We did just that. We had a big breakfast and then played blackjack and roulette. We played some slots and had a few beers. We made some sports bets and played some horses. We took a cab to old downtown Vegas and walked in and out of the casinos. We skipped the show for the evening because it seemed too confining. We were all pumped up about our upcoming job. We stopped and had a steak dinner then headed back to our hotel.

In the room, Paul approached me while I was collecting my thoughts on the balcony.

"At first we may have looked at this job wrong, Mark."

"You know, it's really not a job but part of who we are; who we are as Christians. We are unique with our God given talents and skills."

"None of us could even fathom the torture our Lord had taken on the last day. No one stood up for him which makes me so sick. We have that chance; we will be the ones to free him from all that pain and death. I know this Mark, I prayed about it since I found out about the mission. Once I heard what our mission was, I knew I wanted to go. I would have gone with or without you two. I would and will give my life for Jesus so that he may live. It's not about the money, it's about what's in here," Paul said, pounding his chest.

"I'll take that chance in a machine that I do not completely understand how it operates if it means saving Jesus. If . . . when we save Jesus from the cross, I won't even care if I make it back. No one has had the opportunity or resources to do this job. But we have it now and I will, we will save the Son of God."

I was startled by what Paul had just expressed. It was like he was reading my mind.

Chapter 10

Training

We played over in our minds the interview from the day earlier and the questions and answers. Our conversations finally ended that we would accept this mission, and save Jesus from that cruel death. We were at peace with our answer. Did we miss something? I felt something was missing and I could not put my finger on it.

I felt we possibly overlooked some key questions. We may have not gotten some truthful answers. I could not figure out just why I felt this way and what exactly we were missing. This whole mission was so out of the box, that I just knew that somehow, I possibly didn't ask the right question, or maybe I felt I didn't receive a trustworthy answer.

Laying in my luxurious bed, during the wee hours of the night, I thought about all the help I had received in the past from my information specialist in the Army. It had dawned on me that we had used him many times to dig up in-depth information on some extremely important missions or information I thought we needed on certain aspects of our missions. His title was a civilian intelligence analyst and he held no rank. These specialists are responsible for processing, analyzing, and distributing intelligence on key missions we were assigned to. His name was Darby. That's all I knew him by and he knows me by 'Captain.' We never met face-to-face but when we spoke on the phone, there was a level of comfort, like we had been friends for life. To me, he was gregarious, accessible, and good-natured. I needed him now.

When I called Darby, he answered immediately. "Good afternoon, Captain. What brings you ringing my way?"

"Hey Darby, did you hear, me and my team left the military?"

"No shit Captain, but yes I did hear that." Darby laughed.

"Yeah, we're in Vegas now."

"Stop, if you're calling about borrowing money we have a bad connection," Darby continued laughing. "It must be about 2 am there. I am still in Germany and you know we have a nine-hour time difference."

"Seriously, I need a favor. Jake Lepros, CP Industries, can you find out some information for me? Right now, I have next to nothing on him or his company and we already agreed to do a job for the guy. Can you do that for me?"

"Captain, I would be happy to. Give me a day or two and I will get you anything I can find on him and that organization. Anything for you Cap."

"I really appreciate it. We have about a week's worth of training scheduled before we head out."

"That's fine Cap, I will have something before then."

Unbeknownst to me, Darby wasn't the only one that heard my concerns.

At 0700, the three of us went to the hotel lobby and walked out the front entrance where we loaded ourselves into a soft leather, new car smell, stretch SUV. The aroma itself is soothing and settling. Even though this was the same vehicle we took to our first meeting, we felt more comfortable in it today.

As we did on most of our missions, and as irrational and

mythical as it may be, we brought with us some personal belongings to take with us on this assignment. Yes, even though we were Christians, we were superstitious.

Paul had always carried on his person the laminated poem 'Footprints'. This card had been through so many battles and it was tattered, weathered, and torn, but Paul always found strength when he read it and then prayed. That is one item that he will never let go of.

Sy was awarded the Soldiers Medal. It was awarded to him for heroism not involving actual conflict with an enemy. Sy never talks about it but on leave, while he was in Turkey, a large earthquake hit the region he was in. Sy was near a church when it collapsed and immediately went to help. Single-handedly, he was responsible for saving a priest and pulling approximately twelve other people from the rubble of a church. He keeps that medal close to give him courage.

I have a round challenge coin that was given to me when I was promoted to Captain. Printed on the front of this coin is James 3:13. On the back is the verse, *"Who is wise and understanding among you? Let them show it by their good life, by deeds done in the humility that comes from wisdom."*

I keep this coin close to my heart and it would be rough if I had to leave it behind. I have always leaned on that verse whenever I had difficult decisions I had to make. This mission is one of them.

Our driver was the same guy we had before but he wasn't too talkative today. We checked out the city as we motored through it and into the desert. All three of us were upbeat today and anticipating the training ahead. The ride seemed quicker today for some reason. We arrived at the complex. The SUV stopped at one of the warehouses where we exited the vehicle. Jimmy was at the door to greet us.

In this warehouse, we walked through numerous offices and noticed all different types of equipment spread out in each room. All the rooms had an alphabetic number over the door, the first signs of markings we have seen at this complex. Each office was glass in the front and the rear.

Jimmy stopped at one of the offices, pointed out through the darkened window and said, “This, boys, is where you will be doing most of your training.”

We strained to look out beyond the glass.

With that he flipped a switch and the lights in the warehouse lit up as bright as an afternoon sun. It looked like some type of amphitheater. The offices were all around the training facility each with a bird’s eye view of the playing field. The offices appeared to us like sky boxes at a sporting event. From this vantage point, you could watch the people ‘on the field’. Jimmy also showed us the plectron that hovered over the center of the arena, similar to the ones that hang over a hockey arena. Jimmy said that all training was recorded and it can be and is replayed for all to critique.

Jimmy took us to the ‘locker area’.

“Boys, this is where you will change and shower. When you need to take a break, this is where you will come. You each have your private room and bed. Here, you have every amenity you can ask for. I said you would be treated well and here it is! While you are in training, this will be your home away from home.”

We compared this place more to a fancy spa than a locker room. There never was a barracks that matched up to this place. There were unmanned training tables, hot tubs, and ice tubs, and the kicker, I guess for stress relief, was a waterfall. There was a fresh smell in the air, very relaxing and the color on the walls was soothing.

"As you can see, each of you has a locker and an extremely large locker near the arena. You will keep all your gear together with your weapons. All your personal items will be kept here also."

Sy made a comment that "This is how star athletes are probably treated, not us military guys."

Sy smiled, then put his lips together and was somber. We understood what he meant.

"When you get to Jerusalem, this is how your clothing and weapons should be kept and stored so this is good practice starting right here. Let's get started and get into costume, no camouflage for this mission, just good old clothes from way back when. You all just need to be comfortable in these." Jimmy handed each of us a shoe box. "As you can see when you put your sandals on that they will be the most comfortable in the city... Jerusalem," Jimmy said chuckling.

Paul looked at his sandals and said, "they appear to be old and worn but hey, just put them on, Jimmy's right!" Jimmy explained that the dried-out, shabby pieces of leather we were each given to wear, were scientifically designed sandals. Paul who had already donned his pair, smiled intently while Sy and I worked the sandals onto our feet. These nasty-looking items we had put on our feet looked like road kill. After we maneuvered them onto our feet they felt like an extension of our bodies.

I think Paul was waiting for a reaction, the same that he had after we got the depleted pieces of leather onto our feet.

Yes, we were surprised at how good they felt!

In these sandals we felt the support and comfort that had

been crafted to make this footwear the top of the line, better than any shoe we had ever worn.

I again noticed a monitor in the arena it said JOHN 19:30, with the date and current time. This was another question that still needed to be answered when the time was right.

I noticed the cameras and monitors in all of the offices overlooking the arena. I asked Jimmy if there would be that many people monitoring us during our training.

"Mark, for this mission there will be limited staff due to the secrecy of this event. You see dozens of rooms all around but only about three of them will be staffed."

We changed into our Jerusalem clothing. When we looked at each other, it was so different from the fatigues and camos we were used to seeing that we snickered.

Jimmy led us over to Sid's office. Sid was our trainer. He was a master of the history of Jerusalem in the time of Jesus. Sid was very smart. This mission seemed personal to him. Sid greeted us but rarely looked us in the eyes.

Sid told us that he had been working on his assignment for this mission for the last two years. He had been researching and reading literature on the fundamentals of living during the time of Christ. His notes were vast and encompassed the entire room, in some spots, from floor to ceiling. He had squeezed all his knowledge into a week's summarization, which he needed to share with us. Also, Sid needed us to be our best and that was made possible by giving us as much knowledge he could share and the tools put in place for us to learn.

Looking at his office I could see why Sid always seemed so nervous.

With stacks and stacks of papers and articles, I would be lost and nervous all the time myself, having to work in this environment.

In the Bible, Sid explained, there was no outside interference to rescue Jesus other than Peter's single attempt on the Mount of Olives when the Roman soldiers and the Pharisees came to arrest Jesus.

"Now, we are adding three new people into the picture. You three. This could cause another scenario. As Sir Isaac Newton demonstrated, 'For every action, there is an equal and opposite reaction.' No matter how much stealth you use, your very presence will create an opposite reaction – even if it is only ripple effects, it could be catastrophic. We need to prepare for that.

"There are other groups we need to consider and keep an eye on - the Zealots, the Essenes, and the Believers. Boys, what is written can easily be changed just by you three being there. Each of these groups will be present in Jerusalem, at the same time you will be there. We must prepare for anything and everything."

Sid explained that our outer clothing needed to blend in with the common man in Jerusalem.

"Depending on your status in the community, the quality of your clothing will reflect that difference. People of extreme wealth, in addition to wool, wore garbs of fine lamb skin or leather. Some of the wealthy wore mantels on their shoulders. The middle class wore their tunics just past their knees while the wealthy wore theirs just above the ankle."

"We have designed your clothing of wool of which eighty percent of the people there will be wearing, the middle class. Let me remind you, your tunics are state-of-the-art. From the outside, they look like any other tunic but on the inside, that's a different story. Each of your tunics as you can see, will be worn just below the knees. Your tunics are undyed and a little different from each other again, so as not to attract attention.

"Some of the wealthy you will see have mantels on their shoulders of their tunics. From the mantels, you will see tassels. They wear these to be reminded of the constant presence of the Lord's commandments. The outer belt that they wear, may be decorated with embroidery or precious stones. That's the wealthy; you guys need not worry about that.

"Also, you can see you have cloth for a belt. Sy, your belt is made of cord or rope. Both types need to be tied on your side. It could be loosened or tightened as needed. These belts are designed to prevent flowing robes from interfering with movement from your legs, very common back then. Tighten your belts when you feel there may be a conflict coming your way, just to be prepared."

Sy fumbled with his belt trying to get it into the right position and be comfortable, too.

"You have an inner garment and as you can feel, resembles tee shirt material, cotton."

Paul looked down at his tunic and noticed that the length was somewhat short.

Sid watched Paul and said that the lengths will be adjusted so don't be concerned.

"I will get someone on that today. The other two lengths look fine."

The first thing we had to learn was how to wear our clothing properly so that we did not attract attention. The inside of our tunics was extremely comfortable, with an added thin layer of Kevlar for protection, and wick-away material, and down. They covered it with silk for our comfort.

"The weather conditions we are preparing for are extreme.

If you sleep out at night there will be dampness and humidity. The down will keep you warm in the desert at night and cool during the day. During the day these clothes will offer you dryness and coolness in extreme heat.

"Under no circumstances should you allow any of your clothing to be inspected or, heaven forbid, confiscated. Your clothing is very volatile, so burn if needed. Your clothing needs to look and smell like 2000-year-old clothing but the insides are designed and manufactured like North Face on steroids."

Sid instructed us on how to fold our headpieces and which part of our garb overlapped the other.

"Not too many people at that time had the stature that you three have. The garb will hide some of your bulkiness but not your height. Most males were around 5'5" to 5'7" back then. We believe that Jesus, who was taller than the average, stood out at six feet tall. It would help, when you are out in public, if you three just spread out and tried not to stand together. We anticipated that the soldiers we would send back in time, would be taller than the common man back then, so we designed these garbs with a horizontal design which gives the illusion of someone appearing shorter than they really are."

Sid showed us the weapons we would be taking with us and how to and when to use them. We each were given a knife, military version, made of phosphate carbon steel; a 9mm Sig Sauer handgun with a silencer with two 15-round magazines; a stun gun; tear gas and smoke canisters. All this weaponry was to be kept concealed at all times.

The only weapon to be carried outside the garb would be the *falcata*, a sword-like dagger that was a common weapon for citizens at the time. There were many different swords from different regions made from different materials. Lepros had researched this and poured *beaucoup* bucks into making copies of the one that is kept in the Israel Museum purportedly used during that time period. This was his pet project. Each sword was meticulously made and each was doubled-edged, for about half its length. They were crafted using an iron alloy, weighed about one pound, and were about twenty inches long. Lepros, even though he was urged not to, had the initials CP, inlaid in twenty-four karat gold, on the inner side of each handle.

I thought that since Caesar put his face on coins and forged his name and face on weapons, Lepros wanted to one-up Caesar by putting his signature on this mission.

We each were given medical supplies to be used mostly when we recovered Jesus but for ourselves also, in case we were injured. All three of us were trained combat Medics so we were quite familiar with the medical supplies and how they would be used, which cut down about a day off our training schedule.

We were familiar with all the weapons which also speeded up the training process. Sid also explained to us that the pockets inside our garb would hold and carry all these weapons and the advanced first aid supplies.

Paul knew something wasn't right with his garb. He purposely bent over causing his Sig to fall out and hit the ground. He then stood, extending his arms to his sides, and stared at Sid.

"This is why we have the training, to fix all the bugs that we might encounter," said Sid now noticeably irritated.

Sid stared daggers back at Paul unsure of what he would say next.

"Guys, we have time and all the malfunctions will be remedied."

We even were given money, shekels, that had been

recovered during recent excavations in Jerusalem that date back to the time of Christ.

"An old trait that never died was to haggle over the cost of anything you may purchase. Don't be afraid to negotiate because it could send up a red flag if you didn't. Also, guys, stay clear of the suspicious ones, the ones that look like they are up to no good. Go with your instincts. Watch the beggars because we know many were thieves."

Over the next several days Sid reiterated about the taking of just one life, and how it would affect generations after and strongly advised us not to do so unless it was 'absolutely our last recourse'.

"Taking just one life affects the future lives of their offspring. There would be no offspring! That bloodline ends there. This can affect anyone who is living now. They would disappear if their father or grandfather never lived."

"Whatever means possible!" Sid would say, over and over.

"Anything significant can alter the history books so I beg of you, calculate every move you make."

Our training days consisted of wearing virtual reality headsets and spending hours in the simulators. The 'overseers', the ones in the offices would present or program the different scenarios that we would likely encounter and we learned how to navigate through them. Through these devices, we were able to walk around Jerusalem and engage locals and Roman guards.

Lepros from time to time would stop in and candidly talk to Sid. When Sid finished his conversation with Lepros, each time, he would praise us for learning so quickly and hint that we could begin the mission sooner than anticipated.

I knew wee could do this but I did feel some pressure from

Sid that we should start sooner than planned. Sid was never able to hide his feelings. He would be a terrible poker player.

Our Christian backgrounds easily filled in the blanks in every aspect of the training and task ahead. Numerous events presented themselves to us and we were able to navigate through each one of them. We reenacted different situations where it was plausible to rescue Jesus and get Him to safety. There were circumstances when we believed it would be the best time to complete the mission because the Roman guards would be sparse. Sid cautioned us repeatedly, not to take Jesus unless we could secure his well-being until 3 pm on Good Friday.

We practiced taking Jesus as he rode into town in Jerusalem; we discussed taking him out before or after the last supper. We contemplated that taking out Judas Iscariot before he notified the guards of where Jesus would be. Judas did hang himself so taking his life would have had no effect on the future.

We discussed how to take Jesus out when he was carrying the cross or just before he was crucified. So much of this was up in the air because Sid was not so certain which day or time we would arrive. Even though we were told that it would be within five minutes of the programmed time, Sid decided to allow up to a three to four day window.

I was more comfortable with this training for different scenario arrangements, than dropping in and immediately needing to go do our thing. It gave us options. Naturally, a lot of the training dealt with the Roman Guards and how to respond if needed. We had a reenactment that we were the focal point in the Garden of Gethsemane, Mount of Olives that we felt could be our best opportunity to complete the mission. We would have to take Jesus before the Roman guards came to arrest Him and then keep Him safe until late afternoon on Friday.

Sid dismissed the idea saying that the Roman guards would be all over the place and there would be no way for the three of us to protect Jesus until late Friday. Sid more or less let us put our ideas forward but deep inside, he had his own timetable in mind and preferred to let it play out up until the Crucifixion.

Through extensive conversations back and forth, Sid suggested that we wait until the last possible moment to extract Jesus for 'historical purposes.'

"Even though it may be the best option, it is vital to wait, if possible, up until the Crucifixion. We are training for all circumstances but ideally, we should wait until he is about to be nailed to the cross."

I knew it would be our call when to extract Jesus. We will be there, why should we wait for him to be tortured?

Sid felt differently.

"If we rescue Jesus too early, there would be a very good chance that He would be recaptured and tortured, and crucified all over again. There will be a detachment of Roman soldiers, one-tenth of a legion, a legion being five thousand men, in Jerusalem. In other words, there will be 500 trained Roman soldiers there to maintain order. There is no chance in Hell that you can get Jesus and keep him and yourselves safe for 24 hours. By waiting until the last possible moment, Jesus for sure does not get nailed to the cross at 12 noon, nor does he die at 3 pm. Once you boys return home, and you have kept Jesus from being crucified and, at that time, your mission will have been accomplished. Once 3 pm passes, you guys will be returned home."

My thoughts instantly went to challenge Sid who I surmised

was saying we were not capable of saving Jesus on our time frame. I let those thoughts pass.

Even though now, we were not familiar with all the places to hide Jesus or keep him from the guards, we were confident that we would find a viable location once we arrived in Jerusalem. We had located safe areas occasionally on past missions, I knew we could do it again.

We spent a lot of time practicing how to deal with the locals and the different interactions we might have with them. Just saying 'Hello' was a big deal as to not bring any suspicion on to us. We were also given instruction on telling time with the sun and with the help of a small ancient mechanical device we would be bringing with us, recovered recently from ruins in Israel.

My team took in quite a bit of information. We knew how to blend in and we knew how to keep our mouths shut. Sid was not familiar with special ops at all. He talked to us like we were a bunch of blabbermouths. In my mind, I am thinking, '*Tell us if there is something we need to reply to, otherwise, let us do our job.*'

In the evenings we would read our Bibles and watch replays of our training and discuss ways to improve what we had just trained for.

Paul was concerned with our understanding of the language being spoken. Sy too was not sure how the technology is going to combine with our brains to enable us to understand and communicate.

This is one area that Sid told us we wouldn't get until we were sent back in time. He assured us that the language implants would function flawlessly. Since we couldn't verify this until we got there, it caused me a lot of anxiety. Was there any sort of backup plan if we had a problem with language? We would certainly be identified as strangers, maybe even aliens. Sid had chuckled dismissively and cited the gift of tongues that the apostles experienced at Pentecost. When I tried to press him on this crucial language point, he quoted *Genesis 11:1 "Now the whole earth used the same language and the same words."*

We looked over a current map of Jerusalem and compared it to a map that showed how the city was laid out back then. We marked out comparable points from both maps. One of the most notable landmarks would be the Temple Mount. We all agreed that we would use that location for our center.

We each were given a retrieval device. This tiny device, a ring, was to be kept on us and activated if we needed to be brought back immediately.

"This would be for your safety if you were in imminent danger or injured. We can locate you anywhere with these devices on your person," Sid quipped. There was a place on the side of the ring to activate it for immediate transport. For general information, the ring was solar-powered. It was also a device to signal, 'Mission Accomplished.'

Sid also explained that GPS works with satellites. Since there were no satellites back then, a miniature satellite was installed in each ring designed to have the same results.

I cautiously looked at the rings and could not detect anything out of the ordinary. Paul reassured me that the metal was advanced tech similar to some equipment we have worked with in the field.

"The average person who looked closely at this ring would not be able to detect anything unusual about it. They did a fine job with these as they appear to be just old jewelry," Paul added.

Training went extremely well. We worked late hours so we

were comfortable with every aspect imaginable. We went through scenarios in the city, with the guards, Mt of Olives, the Last Supper, and the Crucifixion. In each scenario, we discussed the best time to take Jesus and get him out. Sid allowed us to train for all the events ahead but he didn't want us to save Jesus until the Crucifixion.

Until we actually get there, we can't be sure exactly at what time we will move to get Jesus out. Sid preferred that we wait until the last possible moment. We have trained for all circumstances. Crowds and guards will heavily factor into exactly just when we complete the mission. Our week of training ended a couple of days early. We must prevent the Crucifixion of Jesus on Good Friday for a successful mission! That's the bottom line!

Our final day was all about the time machine as I called it. Sid referred to it as a time stamp. Six scientists, six of the greatest minds that have developed this software, will be monitoring the entire mission 24 hours a day. The transport back in time and the return only takes moments. Sid explained again that we each lie in a chamber like an MRI machine; every cell of our being and clothing and whatever else we are taking is scanned and processed into this artificial intelligence computer.

Also, pre-scanned into the computer has been every detail of history, the past that we know of, through reference material, books, astronomy, family trees, DNA, eyewitness accounts, languages, and formulas, anything that has ever been recorded including the Bible.

"Your body scans will be merged, incorporated into all this, thusly, you will be placed, blended, at a specific location and place in time, Jerusalem at the time of Jesus Christ. After your mission, when you are recalled to here and now, everything you went there with your person will be returned. Everything scanned will return like when you left to begin the mission. You can't bring anything back that hasn't already been scanned into the computer."

"Are we going to be able to take with us our good luck charms?" questioned Paul.

"The mission you are going on is so significant, that any trace from the future you might bring with you, could destroy the outcome of this assignment. If you were to misplace an item or leave it behind, it would have uncanny results if it were ever found or uncovered at a later date in time. The answer is no."

"That must mean no souvenirs either," said Sy disappointedly.

"Your brains will be returned exactly as it was when it was originally scanned and sorry to say, without any information of your mission. We will know the outcome of your mission by how the current world is altered. Fellas, that is why Mr. Lepros has JOHN 19:30 on the overheads. When that section disappears or changes in the bible, we know your mission has been successful. You will have no recollection because your brains and memory will return to how it was at the time of the original scan when all your information was loaded into the computer. There will be a gap in your memory between when you were scanned and when you return."

"What happens? We get scanned, go to Jerusalem, save Jesus, and return right where we left. We won't remember anything? It's...it's like we never left?" Sy asked.

"Yes, you're exactly right."

"We know this. It has been tested using a simple cell phone and taking photos. On return, the photo is of the time and place that we were sent to. The person who took the photo had no recollection of being there or even taking the photo."

Paul and I were mystified and taken aback. What we just heard was unnerving. We could do a mission but not remember what we had done. There was no getting around this part of the program

"Unfortunately, on this mission, your mission, you will not be allowed to take any device with you other than weapons to complete the mission. We here are more than confident that we will uphold our end, and get you there and back."

Sy and Paul looked at each other and smirked each time Sid referred to the term 'there and back'. I know they are hashing over in their minds the same question I have, "Does this time machine work?"

"You need to make sure you do your part as soldiers. Keep Jesus from being humiliated, tortured, and executed on the cross. You gentlemen have the job that no one has ever done but many have wanted to and that is, "Save the Son God."

Chapter 11

Departure Day

With the training of the past several days behind us, and way ahead of schedule, we were now focused on completing the mission. I asked Sy and Paul to bow their heads.

"Father, this may be our last prayer to you here and now, but we ask you, take us into your hands, and watch over us as we rescue your Son, Our Savior, Jesus Christ, from the brutal torture and death we know has occurred. Please Father, if it is your will, so be it done, Amen."

We stayed the last few nights in the training center because Vegas just was not what the three of us were even thinking about. We decided to conserve our time by not wasting it traveling back and forth to the strip. We followed our usual practice of concentrating and preparing for our mission.

On the morning of the big day, we rose early and ate some breakfast because we weren't sure just when we would eat again. We got dressed and checked our weapons and supplies. We even brought some rations with us just in case. The most important part of the whole outfit we were wearing was our rings. They were designed so as to not stand out and they blended in with our skin tones and the clothing. The rings appeared to be hollowed-out wood with some metal that matched the rings of that time.

As we were dressing, Paul asked me to hand him his ring. It felt much heavier than my ring. I wonder why that would be. Before I could form a question in my mind, Sy entered the room swirling in his robes. The sight of this hulking man cavorting made Paul and I laugh so hard we nearly cried. The distraction cleared some of the apprehensiveness from our minds.

Sid met us in the mess hall and when we were ready, he took us downstairs, and through the tunnel where the time stamp chambers were located. The room looked like a NASA control center. Maps of the Holy City and other logistics were on big screens all across the room. In the center monitor was JOHN 19:30. There were more than 6 people in the room other than us. We received cheerful smiles and subtle hellos from them all. Each of us, one at a time, was scanned separately into the computer. We understood that when we returned this would be the point we would remember. From here on out, we will not recall. I know Sid was extremely nervous and was trying to hide it but doing a poor job at it.

* * *

Muffled sound, *Ring, ring. Ring, ring.* It was Mark's phone emanating from the locker he had just left. The caller, anxiously waited on the other side for him to pick up. It was Darby!

"Come on, come on Cap, pick up the phone."

Darby knew from his experience as an intelligence analyst not to leave important, classified messages on a voice mail.

"Sorry I can't take your call right now but leave a message." Beep.

"This is Mike at Chaz Auto; we found a major problem with your transmission and we need your permission to go ahead with the repairs. Call me back, the sooner the better."

* * *

One of the scientists standing with Sid asked us to follow him to a stage-like area.

"Here is where you guys will leave us for a bit then return here, at this exact location."

I noticed this open area, the time stamp launch area, with markings on the outside perimeter, about eight by eight in size. It's like someone drew a square box on the floor. The floor was highly polished and elevated about a foot off the ground. The lighting was somewhat ambient from the floor to our waistline. There was a more concentrated light, task light, targeting our upper bodies. The room was much bigger than the square we were leaving from. There were no chairs, or other things to rest on. We simply stand there.

"This is called the shoot area, it's a place where you blast off but without a spaceship," said Sid.

In this open room were cameras and what looked to be lasers pointing towards this small area. Lots of lasers! My guess would be possibly thousands with the green tinted light crossing and crisscrossing the launch area.

Sid had told us that this equipment in the launch area is comparable to a 3-D printer but works in reverse. Part by part, our bodies are dissected then merged with all the other data and then we are placed at the final stop which would be Jerusalem.

Sy had been excited about this mission for several days. He was the first of us three to buy into this and he never thought twice about it. Now he was standing there with a big smile on his face that shines through his weeks of growth. He looked like a guy from the time of Christ.

Paul on the other hand had questioned the accuracy of this time machine. He asked me several times about how do we know exactly where we were being deposited and what might we face. Paul said that if we were dropped in the middle of Roman soldiers, our mission would be finished before we even started. He said what if we are off a few years? I tried to be as reassuring as possible. "Paul, we have the rings. If things aren't just right when we get there, we activate them and return and start all over again."

I too had my concerns. Plan A and plan B. I tried to be positive with my guys but also had my concerns. In Afghanistan or anywhere else for that matter you can find some shelter or make it to a friendly border. You could wait until help arrived. It's not the case here. No one else was trained to rescue us if needed. There was no border to run to. We were in God's hands.

This may sound kind of dumb but I didn't put too much into this conversation because I knew when we came back it would be not in our memories. We stepped onto this stage. With that first step onto that platform, I felt that we were leaving the earth for the last time. We didn't look around but looked at each other. Sy no longer had that big grin on his face. It was a sobering moment for us all. We each had beams of lights draped all across our bodies, shimmering and electric.

"Good luck gentlemen, see you in a couple of days," said Sid.

I glanced down quickly to make sure my ring, my return device was on.

"Have a safe trip," one of the scientists blurted out.

Then there was this whooshing sound like we were dropping from the air. I heard talking from the background, familiar voices from the mission control center, then strange voices in a completely different language. I looked down at my ring again and saw my hands and arms glowing. Glancing up I could see

Sy and Paul close by still and glowing too. By the time we could even process these thoughts, we were on solid ground. Looking around, it appeared that we had made it to our destination. I hoped it was the Jerusalem we had been studying but we needed to know for sure. We saw a walled city washed in brown sandstone. The roads were sand and stone, truly primeval looking. The question is, are we here at the time of Jesus? We needed to confer with someone here to be able to tell us if we were in the right place, at the right time.

* * *

Ring, ring. Ring, ring. It was Darby calling Mark's phone again and still in Mark's locker. This time someone picked up the phone; then hung up! All Darby heard was a busy signal. Once more Darby tried but now, the phone was out of service.

Back at mission control, the team was celebrating; celebrating the first time this computer was successful! They had confirmation that we had traveled to the past, to the city of Jerusalem. They were confident that they had the correct dates. They were ready to monitor our location as we traveled about Jerusalem through the tracking devices on our rings. The time stamp machine had sent objects into the past but never a human until now. The time stamp machine also never returned anything from a test mission. Lepros was not concerned about returning us. He only wanted someone to go and keep Jesus from the cross. Lepros did not want anyone to return. He had no intention of returning anyone. In fact, the time stamp machine had not been programmed to return anything.

Little did my team or I know, that this was a one-way mission.

Lepros sat at his desk in his office and watched the control center as we left for this mission. Mark was right, Lepros had other plans. Lepros clapped his hands in a defiant manner, now cursing at God. “It’s my Kingdom now!” he said under his breath. He looked at the monitor in his office where it read JOHN 19:30. From that point on, there was never a minute gone by that Lepros didn’t look up, waiting for that inscription to go away. He would be honed into that for the entire mission.

Lepros summoned Jimmy and thanked him for all his research in locating the three soldiers used for this mission. He degradingly said to Jimmy, “Did you ever think that when you were dishonorably discharged from the service that you would end up being a highly paid handyman doing my dirty work?”

Lepros laughed so hard at Jimmy.

Jimmy was taken back and embarrassed that someone would come out openly and say something like that.

“You are a loser but you don’t have the balls to leave this company because frankly, you love the money you are getting paid. When I am done with you can move on but for right now, go find something to do. Here, take this, a little bonus for bringing those three to me, now get the hell out of here.”

Jimmy got up and as he was walking towards the door, Lepros stopped him.

“Wait, before you go, find me another soldier. One man, one mission. A back up plan. Don’t get me a goody two shoes. I need someone with no heart, a total loser, someone that will go back in time and finish the job if these three can’t. You know what I am talking about?” Lepros laughs again.

Jimmy left the complex dejected. He got in his car and drove to Vegas. He was angry at himself for lowering his standards to work for Lepros. Jimmy always thought that his personality would land him a good job somewhere. He thought Lepros, his

Company and his money, would make Jimmy a better person by getting him into a higher quality position with the company. Jimmy never knew that he was hired because he was vanquished, a defeated person. Jimmy had been employed by Lepros now for over two years. Lepros hired Jimmy because he was a bomb expert in the military; he was a disgruntled bomb expert. Jimmy was dishonorably discharged because he attempted to sell explosives to an undercover agent in a sting operation.

A deal was later reached in court and the charges against Jimmy were dropped. Jimmy hooked up with Lepros about the same way he located Mark, Paul and Sy. When Jimmy met Lepros, he was hired to find soldiers capable of pulling off this mission. Jimmy became Lepros' recruiter.

Through some connections, Jimmy was able to obtain lists of soldiers with certain criteria. He was looking for soldiers with no dependents and no known home addresses. Surprisingly, the list was quite extensive. The other prerequisite was who was getting out of the service during the time period that Lepros had established.

These three were all leaving at the same time and were highly trained. The captain and his team were the perfect candidates. Jimmy was notified by his confidential source just when they were going to separate from the service and and where they were headed. The rest was history, only Jimmy didn't realize just how close he would get to the three of them. Over the last couple of weeks, Jimmy bonded with the three soldiers. He became close to each one of them and didn't want their relationship to end.

Despite being such an outgoing person and all, Jimmy never had any real friends. He was too conniving, and untrustworthy.

Over the last several days though, Jimmy had become attached to the three boys. Each day he became closer to them, and each day he regretted what he was doing. Jimmy knew he was betraying these guys. He led his three new friends into the mouth of the lion. Jimmy knew of the mission soon after he himself was hired. He knew that when the time stamp was completed his friends would be sent into the past to a death sentence.

Back at his room in Vegas and collecting his miserable thoughts, a Bible, that had been perched on the table, was open. Jimmy looked down and read it.

Matthew 26:14-16 Then one of the twelve-the one called Judas Iscariot went to the chief priests and asked. "What are you willing to give me if I deliver him over to you?" So, they counted out for him thirty pieces of silver. From then on Judas watched for an opportunity to hand him over.

Jimmy poured a drink and wept!

Chapter 12

Passover in Jerusalem

So, this is Jerusalem, the City of David! It looks much different than Sid explained and how he described it would be while we were preparing for this mission. I was expecting arid desert-like conditions. I know we are now in a different place than we had been just moments ago. It's sunny but everything looked like it was well watered, spring-like, green. The air felt fresher, much cleaner than where we had come from. The climate is more temperate. We were now standing on sandy ground totally surrounded by flowery bushes and a few trees. The perfect drop, if we were in the right place. I guess sending us here was like they were dropping a Humvee out of a plane. They weren't sure it would end up in the right place.

Sy whistled and then said, "Wow."

Looking out from our elevation we saw oceans of wildflowers filling the slopes leading to the valleys below then cresting back up to the hills in the distance. The trees were blossoming, and the entire area as far as we could see was green. The lands lay textured in what appeared to be orchards and vineyards. We were not in Nevada anymore.

Both Sy and Paul were mesmerized as they looked out from our well-hidden out-of-the-way location. Paul closed his eyes and pulled in an expansive breath. Sy continued to have a fixed gaze on the hills.

It felt like a dream to me. It felt like I had fallen asleep and woke up in a dreamland, possibly even heaven.

Behind us, were the sandstone walls. We could see the tops of some buildings peering out behind the wall. As the sun glistened upon the great walls, they revealed to us their spectacular rosy-golden glow.

Looking through the bushes, we saw numerous sheep in the distance; some running freely while others in flocks were controlled by a shepherd. Shepherds, our first sign of human life. They were dressed in plain-looking tunics. The tunics looked dirty, most likely from attending to the flock. They wore sandals and their heads were wrapped in what appeared to be some type of woven woolen cloth. Each of them carried a stick much longer than they themselves were, and used that instrument, pushing and prodding, to control the flock in their care.

From our location, we could see donkeys tied to wooden posts outside the walls. There were no street lights or overhead wires. There were no signs either which made our job more intriguing, thereby causing us to lean more on history and the sun for a road map.

I needed to know where we were, exactly. I needed some kind of confirmation that we were in Jerusalem, in the time of Our Lord. My heart was pounding in dire uncertainty. It is just the three of us now and I need to feel at ease knowing we are where we are supposed to be. I need control.

We had landed in a secluded area not far from the city walls. We heard people talking and laughing, and as we looked out through the bushes we saw lots of people traffic coming and going towards and away from those walls. We heard the bray of a donkey and the sounds of wheels turning on a stone road. A few people pulled hand carts. These carts had long extended handles that protruded from the cart all the way past the person pulling it, much like carrying a stretcher. In the cart itself were goods. Some people were pulling full carts holding some type of fruit, while others we saw were pulling wood, and furniture. Some people were carrying different items on their backs. Children too seemed to be assisting the others carrying various items under their arms. One child had a cage and a rope draped over his shoulder with what appeared to be a chicken inside.

We walked a few steps from the brush to a road and followed the people toward the walls. We gradually spread out about a half-block distance from each other and were able to keep full eye contact with one another.

The road we were now on led to a double-arched gate surrounded by the walls. I took several deep breaths, hoping this was Jerusalem. Most of these people we see here are heading in the same direction, into the gates. Sy and Paul look to me as their leader. I cannot let them down now being so unsure if this is our destination.

"Excuse me," stopping a man on the road, "Is this Jerusalem?"

The man paused and looked at me.

"The City of David?"

"Oh yes, it is," he said with a smile, "Shalom."

"Shalom to you."

I pressed my hand to my heart and looked up to the sky,

"Thank you, God," I whispered quietly.

I motioned to the guys with a thumbs up. They each nodded their heads and continued walking.

Based on the location of the sun, the gate we were

approaching was facing the east. Sid had mentioned this location.

"This gate if you can find it, is referred to as the 'Golden Gate.'"

Suleiman the Magnificent sealed this gate in 1541 A.D. to prevent the Messianic prophecy of Zechariah 14:4. '*that in the Day of Yahweh's Coming the Mount of Olives will be split in half from east to west*'.

The Church fathers believed that when Jesus returns, He will enter through this gate. The sealing of the opening was to prevent the fulfillment of this prophecy. Most of our mission would be in and out of this gate as it is believed that Jesus passed through this gate several times this week, coming and going to the Kidron Valley and the Mount of Olives.

We are in the right location; but is this the right time?

As we got closer to the entrance of what we now knew wass Jerusalem, the mixed smell of burning wood and cooked meat filled the air.

We entered through the gate, and past the large walls that surrounded the city. We walked amongst many entering, yet heard many more voices from within the city. It was festive. We heard people singing and chanting. As we approached the Temple area, the crowd became denser. By the smiles and some laughter, we could tell people were having a good time. There were hundreds of people in this area. The ground was sandy which may have accounted for the dust in the air. Most people were unphased by the sand but Paul had placed his scarf closer to his mouth and nose to eliminate some of the particles in the air. Sy didn't seem to mind the air quality at all.

Inside the city walls, were hastily assembled wooden huts for vendors, spread out as far as one could see.

Paul, who was several feet away, motioned for me to look ahead. We noticed in the distance that objects were being tossed in the air. As we worked our way closer, we discovered it was a man looking straight up in the air, unphased by the crowd that had gathered around him, methodically juggling melons.

Each booth or hut had different products being offered to the people. In one location, they were selling food, bread, and slices of unknown meat. Next to the meat hut, hanging on the wall, was a dead camel. I could only guess what type of meat they were preparing and selling. Several of these huts had fruit as their number one item. There were many types of grapes and figs for sale.

Sy looked intrigued at all the different vendors as he went from one hut to the next. There were nut vendors selling fresh walnuts. Others selling olives, pomegranates, and oranges. Some vendors had no enclosures and were walking around vending scarves and rugs. Outside of a large shoddy and dirty-looking tent, men were trying to get attention by using puppets as a pretense to lure people inside.

Other huts were still being constructed and goods were being placed within them as they were being completed.

There were sheep, goats, chickens, and dogs roaming freely, everywhere. Some of the sheep walked in a small herd; others were being carried over people's shoulders in sacks still alive and kicking. Once we located the great temple, we easily got our bearings.

We needed to find out when or if Jesus was arriving or if he was there already and determine what the exact date was now. Are we early? Is it too late? Are we even in the right year? We needed to confirm if the computer delivered us to the right time in history.

We knew that people were here from all over the world to celebrate Passover in Jerusalem. Sid had told us that every continent would be represented, and he was right. We noticed many people dressed as we were but we also noticed others that were not. We were not out of place. We saw people wearing large strands of gold draped around their necks and exotic jewelry, massive stones clinging from their ears. Not only the clothing and jewelry were different, but how some people wore their hair. Most had long hair and very few showed their bald heads. Some had trinkets in their hair like sticks and birds' nests and one woman had an entire bouquet cropped on top of her head. There were different lengths of beards and growth so we didn't feel out of place. The three of us had about a week's worth of facial hair. There were many people of different colors.

Walking through the city we heard people speaking different languages. I was concerned that we would be stuck in the middle of Babel. Fortunately, as Sid had predicted, the computer translator chips worked. Passing different groups of people, we heard each conversation in our own native language. That was a huge relief.

We walked back towards the Temple and through the crowds maintaining a good distance apart from each other. We tried not to stand out but we must have looked like tourists or something because an older chubby man approached me. Out of nowhere, with hundreds of people around, this guy singled me out. His eyes were like fire yet his voice was calming and charming. He was clean-shaven and wore a clean tunic, a bit whiter than most.

He reminded me of 'gramps'. Gramps was in one of my homes while I was in foster care. Gramps was the guy you would run to, to be rewarded and hugged. He always made it a special deal to celebrate our small successes like getting a good grade in school or building a birdhouse at home. On the other hand, you didn't want to be around Gramps if you did something bad like get in trouble at school or steal one of the other foster kid's belongings. Gramps would be intimidating, rolling up his sleeves before he unleashed and made an example of you. He would rant and rave until you broke down and cried. He continued until you showed remorse. Yes, this guy had Gramps's eyes and I am sensing that personality also.

I have always watched a person's hands when they approach me and while speaking to them. Their hands will always reveal their true intentions. A person with clinched fists, maybe talking nicely, but inside there is anger; if they have fidgety hands, it usually indicates they are not being honest.

This man approached with hands as calm as could be, a sign of honesty.

"You must be from out of town," he stated.

During this brief conversation he inadvertently directed each hand pointing in one direction which might indicate to me, this guy is either trying to control my situation or he has something to show me or sell me.

"Why would you guess that old man? Isn't everyone here from out of town?"

He laughed at my quick comeback. I thought to myself, "Man, this guy is slick, he's much like Jimmy with that smile and guts to just walk up to me and say what's on his mind."

"Are you here for Passover and to see the preacher, Jesus of Nazareth?" Without waiting for a response, he said, "Some say he is the Son of God; others say he is a blasphemer."

My heart beat harder, I looked up to the heavens, my heart

was smiling but I didn't want to show my relief outwardly.

"Of course, we came to hear Jesus!"

Inside I exalted, I knew we were in the right place, finally getting confirmation.

I wanted to yell out to the other two, "We made it."

Did I just hear him say see Jesus? Pinch me! I am really here and Jesus is somewhere right around the corner. That is when reality struck me. We actually made it! I wanted to scream out loud in joy but somehow contained it. I felt like I was smirking, my heart was smiling. Our destination has been confirmed. My mind now needed to focus on the mission.

"Well, I have some connections here, how about I help you find a place to stay while you are here? Would a few nights work out for you? There are... three of you, correct?" the old man hesitantly asked.

I thought he must have seen us together earlier because we were not together when he approached me and we were not together now.

"Yes, three."

I asked him if Jesus has arrived.

"Yes, he is here. Jesus has been giving sermons daily up on the Mount," he said pointing in the direction of the Mount of Olives.

Paul and Sy gathered closer as I spoke to the man.

"A place to stay would be great. By the way, what's your name?"

"Gabe," he said with a smile.

"I'm Mark, that's Paul and Sy, over there," pointing to each man as I introduced Gabe to them.

"Let me check around for a place and I will find you boys, go and explore. You'll find Jerusalem full of interesting sights, especially this time of the year."

If Gabe could spot us as out-of-towners, what about others, what about the Roman guards? I admit we were a little bigger than the everyday people walking around but some of the guards looked intimidatingly large as well. I just did not want any type of showdown between us and the Roman Empire unless and until it was necessary. As I looked around, I saw so many different types of people. We don't look any different than any of them. I needed to stop worrying. I needed to settle down. How could I? We were going to see Jesus.

We stayed apart but near each other, so as not to attract any more attention to ourselves. We set off to explore the city.

Sy seemed interested in the vendors and he stopped at just about every booth with a look of innocent curiosity on his face. He found a guy doing some carny tricks. This guy had three hollowed-out shells and placed a customer's shekel under one of them and moved them around. The person who provided the shekel pointed to where it might be. If he was right, he would get two shekels in return. If he was wrong, well, he lost it. Sy watched for a long time and figured out the man with the shells would swipe the shekel and there wouldn't be a coin under any shell causing that person to lose a shekel. Each person trying this game experienced a loss. However, on the third try, they would win. They were scamming people back then! We call it three-card Monty, they called it three-shell shekel.

Paul was just fascinated with the city itself and the architecture. It seemed so different than what he had anticipated. He was expecting stone and sand but there was plenty of wood which surprised him. Painting and carvings were something he never believed he would see. Doorways and some walkways were trimmed with ornate wood. As Paul was gazing at some artwork, he was suddenly sideswiped by a Roman on horseback and knocked to the ground. The Roman turned briefly to look at Paul and let out a chuckle as he and his horse trotted forward.

I was focused on the mission. Relieved we were here at the right time in history, and only revved up my attitude in making this a successful assignment.

In some situations, like confronting a vendor, it was just like the simulator, in other situations, it was different. Surprised, one woman sobbed trying to sell me a scarf. When I firmly declined, she immediately stopped crying turned to the next potential customer, and began wailing again. There were many beggars on the walkways and many appeared to be handicapped. The Roman soldiers we walked past didn't appear too observant; some were propped against a wall with their eyes closed. Some of them were just wandering on and not appearing to be flexing any muscle.

I stood near a wall looking at all that was going around this Passover week. Still somewhat in a daze, and in disbelief that we were here, my mind raced as I prepared mentally for the mission that was ahead.

"Mark! Mark!"

Who could be calling? Should I even turn around? I don't know anyone here.

It was Gabe. When he got closer, he reached out and grabbed my sleeve to get my attention.

"I found a place for you boys right on the main square not too far from here. Do you want to take a look?"

I motioned for the other guys to follow me as I walked with Gabe. We walked to this small stone apartment at the ground level. It was tight for the three of us but it also was a great place to be, right in the heart of all the festivities. There was one doorway and one tiny window. The ceiling of the apartment was tall with two air ventilation openings near the top. The place was bare basic and a bit dusty from the sandstone floor. It also had a small fireplace and a fresh bundle of wood next to it. We could smell the aroma from the wood as we entered the place. It seemed like a good property but we had nothing to compare to. We are military guys. We sleep where we need to. We stay warm where we can. There were no complaints from Sy or Paul. Gabe smiled at my approval and said that it was only a few shekels.

"From here you will be able to get a good look at the preacher."

I held out my hand with some shekels and Gabe took what was needed. Paul and Sy tried to squeeze through the door simultaneously and stopped for a moment, stuck in the narrow doorway looking at each other, smiling. Gabe chuckled at the sight, told us to have a good day, and that he would check in on us from time to time to see if there was anything that we might need. This was the first time since we arrived that we could sit back and take all this in.

We hadn't done much but we were all exhausted. As we settled in, there was a knock at the door. We had taken our weapons and gear off from our tunics. I asked the guys to cover them. I was fearful that somehow our cover had been blown. I was worried that maybe the Roman guards were here to take us away.

I carefully went to the door and opened it slightly. It was Gabe again. I let out a huge breath. Sy and Paul both shook their heads and closed their eyes. Then they laughed.

Either he was Jerusalem's best one-man welcoming

committee, or his minions will slit our throats tonight. He seemed like the perfect host, . . . was he too perfect?

"Boys, here are some things for you to eat and drink. You must have had a long journey. If you are looking for Jesus, I was told that he is up at the Mount of Olives."

Sy asked, "Gabe, when did Jesus arrive in town?"

"He arrived last Sunday and received a great welcome. He has many followers you know. He entered the city on a colt. People lined the streets and placed palms on the ground in front of Him."

Paul chimed in, "How many days ago was that?"

Gabe, looking somewhat confused at the question replied, "...three, why?"

We thanked him for the food and information on Jesus. Gabe smiled and left as fast as he arrived. We all thought that Gabe seemed to be very sincere. The way he spoke to us, was very calming and the attitude he had towards us was comforting. He seemed to be looking out for us.

Gabe had brought us some bread, cheese, and wine. We sampled everything first, then, devoured the entire meal. We are definitely not connoisseurs of fine food but I must say this was some of the freshest, finest-tasting food we had ever eaten. We all have had cheese from Wisconsin but this cheese here was indescribably creamy and tasty. The wine was so smooth and did not affect how we felt. I don't know the alcohol content, but it must be quite low. The bread was just out of the oven because it was still slightly warm. The perfect snack!

We gathered our things and then headed over to the Mount to get a look at Jesus. The three of us split up and we walked through the crowds and past the Golden Gate.

On the road to the Mount, stopped up ahead, were four

Roman guards on horses. As we got closer, we watched them detaining people and questioning them as to where they were heading. They each had a long javelin-type armory that they used to jostle people and shove them away. We decided that this was not the time to try and make it past them. Surely one of us would be stopped and questioned. We decided to return to our quarters. From our distance, none of us saw Jesus or anyone preaching on or near the Mount. We did not even see a crowd gathering there either. The crowd appeared to have been stymied by the Roman check point.

We returned to our apartment. We sat on the floor and brought up the mission.

"This is it guys, we're here."

"There were some strange-looking people at the festivities," Sy said, grabbing his stomach and chuckling.

"I don't want to be a party pooper but guys, I am exhausted. Could we talk about it in the morning?"

"Are you ok?"

"Yea, just tired," said Paul.

When we woke, Sy threw some wood in the fireplace to get it going and take some of the chill out of the air.

"What do you guys think about Gabe?" Sy blurted out.

Paul was half awake lying on the floor and replied sarcastically. "He has been extremely accommodating. Look at our surroundings."

Paul raised both arms in the air while Sy laughed hard.

"He seems good-hearted and sincere."

"Let's not let our guards down guys. You know how the Afghans turned on us after saying that they love Americans...not to mention the Iraqis and others. We learned the hard way. Let's not get trapped into some false sense of security."

I felt that maybe there was something more about Gabe. I couldn't put my finger on it. I didn't quite understand but I was certain, Gabe was not an enemy.

We dressed in our garb that had been designed 2000 years in the future. We meandered cautiously out the door. Already, even this early in the morning, the crowd was extensive yet seemed very upbeat. The people had gathered and began preparing more food. The fires were lit and the aroma of burning oak spread across the entire area. The vendors were restocking their booths with food and wares. People were laughing. A few of the people had instruments, a bowl harp, much like a modern-day guitar, and were strumming the cords making some kind of music. These instruments caught my eye as it appeared they used tortoise shells as resonators and a bent stick for a neck and about three or four silk strings. The sounds were intriguing and upbeat.

Again, we spread out but stayed in close proximity to our little refuge. Two young kids possibly eight or nine were playing some sort of game in the street near our room. They were throwing a cloth object around, chasing it and each other. We stood and watched.

Somehow Sy got involved in the game with them which made Sy laugh and the boys also. One of the boys had thrown this object and indivertibly it headed towards Sy.

"Watch it!" he shouted then laughed uncontrollably.

Sy quickly ducked which caused even more laughter by his quick quirky reflexes. When Sy tried to ignore them after that, they started teasing Sy to get his attention again. Sy jokingly tried to dismiss the boys but they became more energetic the more Sy ignored them. The boys started laughing so loud that a nearby door opened and a woman appeared.

She shouted at the boys, “Rufus, Alexander,” and she seemed a bit embarrassed. Seeing that Sy was right there in the middle of the two boys, she approached Sy.

“Sir, I am so sorry that my sons have intruded on your privacy.”

“On behalf of the boys,” Sy responded, smiling, “they were playing quietly in the street when I joined in. I should be the one to apologize. I was the one that fueled their wildness and uncontrolled laughter.”

Sy felt uncomfortable, in a good way.

While speaking to this woman Sy was sizing up the situation and trying not to focus on the beauty this woman possessed.

“These two boys are mine. I was taken aback to hear them laughing. Since their father died over a year ago, they have been pretty quiet and not very outgoing.”

Sy extended his condolences to the lady. Sy and the woman never seemed to break eye contact.

Paul and I were nonchalantly watching. I thought that Sy needed to end this conversation. He needs to dismiss it and move on. It doesn’t appear this is happening at all. Sy seemed zoned in talking to this woman.

“Please,” the woman said apologetically, “come and have something to drink, this is where we are staying for Passover,” as she motioned Sy over to her dwelling.

She asked Sy where he was staying and to her delight, he said he was staying right next door. She stopped for a moment then turned to Sy and introduced herself.

“I am Veronica.”

Sy introduced himself and added with a smile on his face, “It’s so nice to meet you.”

Both Veronica and Sy beamed. Sy unconsciously started fiddling with his hands while Veronica kept moistening her lower lip.

Well, 'Hells Bells' I have never seen Sy, in all these years together, fall head over heels with a woman, more or less a two-thousand-year-old woman. It could have been in my head but I think that both Sy and Veronica were flirting. Sy stayed outside her dwelling and she reappeared with some type of drink. Sy and Veronica talked for a great deal of time. Whenever the two boys tried to interrupt their conversation, Veronica sent off them each time.

I began to think of some way to distract Sy and have him rejoin us.

Paul was watching as closely as I was. When their conversation finally ended, Sy looked up at us and turned to go into our building. Paul and I followed him back to our residence and inquired as to his conversation with 'The Lady.' Sy said that her name was Veronica. She had come here from a faraway place for the Passover Celebrations.

"I told her I too came from a faraway place. I also told her I was staying with two friends,"

Sy explained that their conversation was pretty superficial. Sy was exasperated by our probing.

"Do you think I'm dumb enough to tell her that we were from the future?"

When we looked at each other and shrugged, Sy waved a dismissive hand at us.

Later in the afternoon, while the three of us were inside, Gabe again showed up.

"Boys, can I speak with you for a minute, it's quite urgent?"

He had our attention. Maybe this was what we were waiting

for.

"I have a message."

'From who' I thought, 'there is no one here that knows of us, maybe mission control sent something.'

"I know why you boys are here."

Hearts pounding, blood pressure up! Minds racing!

"My message is from our Creator. God would like you to reconsider the reason why you came here."

We were blown away. Who is Gabe really? How does he know why we are here? What does Gabe really know?

"You came here for the love of Jesus the Christ did you not? You have a motive for being here; but maybe it's not the purpose you were intended to come here for, but maybe it's for another reason. I am asking you boys to open your hearts and your minds and listen to what I am telling you; what God is telling you. Leave it be. This message has been delivered."

Gabe looked each one of us in the eyes then turned and left.

We were speechless and unprepared for that.

Gabe had just given us a directive from the highest level.

"If it's not the mission what is the 'purpose' of why we are here? If God allowed us to be transported to Jerusalem, what was His reason for bringing us here?"

Paul and Sy who had both been overly quiet since we got here chimed in. Sy was somewhat startled, "What was that all about? Maybe we 'should' reevaluate this whole thing, Captain. It's giving me the creeps."

"Guys let's not jump to any conclusions about any of this. We have only known Gabe for a day and we are worried about the message he brought us. Who is Gabe anyway? It's possible that Gabe doesn't know anything about our mission. He may believe that we're here to hurt Jesus instead of saving Him?

Don't let what some old geezer said get into your heads."

" I don't believe our mission control center sent him to watch over us. But if they did, they would have told us they were sending a fourth person. Guys, we have no idea if anything has changed. We don't know anything other than what we were trained to do, period. Gabe is just guessing why we're here. Maybe he works for someone else to gather information on the visitors, who knows?"

"There could still be other ways to get the mission done that we haven't thought about like, maybe we can just alert the apostles as to what is going to happen since they really didn't know the fate of Jesus until the trial. Then they can take Jesus and get him out of harm's way. Take him from the city."

"Paul, stay focused on our mission. Stay focused on what we trained and practiced for. Don't get sidetracked. Sid reminded us to let history play out as long as possible. Alerting the apostles was not one of the scenarios that we trained or practiced for. There will be some road bumps and this is probably one of them but let's not get off course."

"We need to separate Jesus from the Cross, and that's our mission. We have gone through numerous scenarios. Alerting the apostles was not one of them. They would want to know how we knew and that's not going to happen, period."

"But the results would be the same," Sy said, "then our mission would be complete, no?"

"Guys" I said, "we will complete this mission as we had planned. No ifs, ands, or buts. Got it!"

Sy got a little agitated and not his normal calm self. He tightened up his muscles and he looked like he was about to burst. Sy got up and walked out the door as he was not used to being talked to the way I had spoken to him.

Paul stayed back and tried to reason with me.

"We accepted this job for one reason and one reason only, to save Jesus. I'm starting to feel resistance not from the soldiers but from my heart. I need to know that I'm doing the right thing."

"Talking about this mission back home is one thing, but being here and completing it is another. I agree with you Paul that this is a very emotional undertaking unlike any we ever could have imagined. This assignment that we have accepted, would and will affect Christianity and humanity as we have never seen."

I shared with Paul the feelings I had about Lepros and how it contradicted what was in my heart.

"I agreed to accept this mission not because of Lepros or the money end of it, but who we were saving. It is still tearing me apart inside."

Paul listened intently. When we finished the conversation Paul said he was going outside to join Sy. I nodded and turned away from Paul. As much as we had discussed this mission before, I still needed my time to think about and digest this mission and put everything back into perspective. The three of us had trained hard but had not given enough thought about the spiritual end of things. Paul walked off on his own, the first time any of us were apart since Vegas.

When Sy took off, he went straight to Veronica's. Sy left with an attitude but that quickly changed when he saw her. They both began their conversation about Jesus. Veronica emotionally said that she hadn't seen him yet.

"I'm looking so much forward to hearing him preach."

"That's why I am here also."

Veronica asked Sy if he had ever heard of a country called

Phut just west of Egypt.

"That's where I am from. My husband was a soldier. He carried his shield and bow. He fought and won battles in Persia and Lud. He came back telling stories he heard of this man, Jesus, who had performed miracles. Jesus brought people back from the dead and cured the sick. He expressed the need to see Jesus but died before he could. I promised myself that I and my boys would see and hear Jesus no matter what. We started this journey to the City of David, to hear the preacher, to hear possibly, the Son of God."

"Do you believe he is indeed the Son of God?" asked Sy.

"I want to believe but I want to see Him and hear Him speak. I would truly know then."

During their conversation, Sy became even more intrigued by Veronica. Her beauty alone captivated him.

Veronica asked Sy where he was from. This took Sy back and he was nervous about answering.

"I too am from a faraway land, but not Phut. I would like to one day have a ranch and raise some cattle," he said evasively with a little hoarseness in his voice. That brought a smile to Veronica's beautiful face.

Sy had never had a good female relationship, a long-time female relationship. None of us had! Sy never had that chance, from foster care to the military. He finally is free and seems to be head over heels for Veronica. Sy had made some moves to get closer to Veronica while they were talking. Veronica seemed to be smiling at nothing while he was talking. They both displayed that yearning look. The look of love.

We have a mission that tops all missions, saving Our Lord, Jesus Christ, and Sy seems happy and content. As religious and devoted as Sy is, and so inspired when this job became available,

I am surprised at how lightly he seems to be taking on our mission now. Usually, Sy is the logistics guy. Sy wants to know who, what, when, where, and why. Sy wants to know our options. On this mission, I am missing that part of Sy.

Paul returned and apologized for how he was handling all this. With his humor, he said, "It must be the jet lag."

We both chuckled as it broke some of the tension we were all feeling. I told Paul that we needed to walk around some more, check some areas and map things out a little better so it would be clearer for us when we made our move. When we do actually have Jesus, we needed to find a location that we could bring him to, a safe zone, at least for a while.

We would need to tend to his medical needs and we need to have the cooperation of some if not all the apostles. What is written in the Bible on how the apostles either denied knowing Jesus or ran in fear of persecution, made us wonder how much of a help they actually would be. We talked about this in preparation for this mission with Sid and that is why he suggested taking Jesus just before getting nailed to the cross. We would only need to protect Him until the 'Final Hour' had passed, then history would ultimately be rewritten.

Chapter 13

Getting the Lay of the Land

Paul and I left our quarters and after about 30 minutes of roaming around the outer gates of Jerusalem, we ran into an old man with water by the cistern. It's possible that he maybe ran into us. It was getting warm. We needed a drink and the Cistern was inviting. It appeared to be very welcoming just by the way people were acting around the cistern. People were dancing and joking around with each other. A man and a woman each had a large palm branch in their hands and were swinging them at each other laughing. This highly visited place outside the walls was an oasis for the thirsty. Others that were gathered there were cheerful and talkative. A child with a bucket started to play in the water causing her mother to scold her playfully. The cistern was a gathering place. People came and filled their jugs with water and share stories of the day.

With the palms of his hands raised to the sky, an elderly man graciously offered us a drink and he asked us if we needed help with finding anything. We filled our lambskin containers and asked him about Jesus of Nazareth.

"Oh, the Preacher," he exclaimed. The man hurriedly covered up his water container clapped his hands together and happily said, "Follow me."

He reached out and grabbed Paul's arm and led us to a

stand-alone two-story structure outside the walls of the city not too far from the cistern. All the houses in this area were one story so this one stood out just by its height. The outside walls of the building were stone and whitewashed in some type of light stucco, very well maintained.

Whispering in hushed excitable tones he said, "This is where Jesus will be tomorrow fellas. If you would like to get a glimpse of him, just hang out around here. There will be many others here wanting to see him also, so get a good seat. He has many followers."

"Are you sure this is where He will be?"

"There are Passover festivities planned tomorrow evening here in the upper room so I know he will be here." Whispering and looking around, *"I know a few people on the inside. He will be here!"*

Being unable to stand still, and biting down on his smile, he continued on.

"You know we celebrate the Jewish peoples' miraculous exodus from Egypt. I am not a Jew but I know the name 'Passover' comes from the story of the tenth plague, the death of the firstborn, which passed over the Israelites' houses, sparing their children."

My eyes felt like they were glowing. Not paying too much attention to what the guy was now saying, I was focused on the house. I realized that this was the 'Cenacle' the place where Jesus had the Last Supper. We told the old man we were not invited guests but just wanted to see the Preacher.

I told him that we have tried to locate him at several different places but had been unsuccessful. It seemed to me that somehow, it feels like we were purposely being diverted from coming in close proximity to him. Either the Roman Guards cut us off or our timing has been off. On the other hand, maybe we were just given the wrong information.

"Well," he said rubbing his hands together, "you will need to come back tomorrow evening when he will be here."

In my mind, I know this is a mission and it's strictly business, however, just speaking the name Jesus, knowing he is here, here close by, messes with my thought process as a soldier, and a leader and a Christian. Our King, Our Savior, here now, walking amongst us. I want to see him, I need to see Him, but I also needed to focus on the mission; to concentrate on the mission. Paul and I returned to our Jerusalem Hotel and Sy was still not back yet.

Sy was out with Veronica. Paul and I discussed that if we didn't locate Jesus tonight, we would find Him at that house tomorrow. Once we have made contact, we can stay near Him until we make the extraction.

I was conflicted because we wanted to be near Him now.

I questioned Paul saying, "We have located so many people in the past so why are we having this much trouble getting to Him or even near Him? Locating Jesus sooner than later will help us determine what action we need to take and when."

"That's a good question, Cap."

Later in the day, Sy returned. He had a bounce to his step. He put his hand on the back of Paul's shoulder while smiling at me. "Good evening to you all!"

Paul's body posture perked up, surprised at Sy's playfulness.

I told him that 'we', meaning, the three of us, were going out to locate Jesus and make preparations to complete our mission. I reminded Sy that he was and always will be our logistics guy and that we need him here and now with total focus on this mission.

We told Sy that the last supper is tomorrow and we had located the house. He put his head back briefly, then put his fists together cracking one set of knuckles, then the other. "I am ready, Captain, let's do it."

My question to the guys was, "Should we take Jesus out tomorrow?"

"It might be our best shot, maybe the easiest time to get Him. We could take Jesus out before or after the supper depending on how many people are around and how many guards there are," said Sy shaking his head.

"Before dinner, Jesus will have a big crowd around him. So that won't be an option," Paul fired back.

I got impatient with Sy. I had created a mental tally of what could go wrong. Taking Jesus out before the Last Supper was never an option.

"We also need to consider, if the situation arises, taking out the apostle Judas. Judas was the one person we can easily take out with no one ever thinking anything about him because he is going to commit suicide anyway. Once we neutralize Judas, we could render the aid of the apostles to get Jesus out of there and we could join them to escape. We would somehow create a sense of urgency among the eleven, to help us rescue Jesus. We need to get them motivated to assist."

Sy fidgeted, looking back and forth between us and the door.

"We could tell them that someone just killed Judas, and they're coming for the rest of them."

"After dinner," Paul said, staring us both in the eyes, "we know Jesus will be by himself for a little while when three of his apostles will be sleeping."

Sy rubbed his forehead.

"I like the idea of stopping Judas. After Judas sold Jesus to the Pharisees for thirty pieces of silver, he immediately regretted his decision and soon after, hung himself. We would just be beating Judas to the punch. There would be no Mount of Olives, no Garden of Gethsemane, no arrest, no torture, and no Crucifixion."

Paul acknowledged that and sat down with a smile and said, "Now that's what I'm talking about, Captain."

Sy and Paul both suggested that we take Jesus to the safe area, the place we first arrived at when we got here. It was somewhat secluded and yet close enough from the city.

"We probably can keep Him there, with us for a full day which would render our mission a success."

I looked at Sy. The expression on his face soon changed. He began sputtering. His body eased up, his shoulders hunched over, and out of the blue he said, "I know, I need to get my mind off her and on this mission, to concentrate. I know I can't bring her back with me."

Sy looked back and forth between Paul and me.

"We share so many of the same beliefs about Christianity and life. And if you are asking, no I haven't, I can't tell her where I came from and what I am about to do. I am torn because I am loyal to our team and our mission but I am also in love."

After each of us had collected our thoughts and calmed down some, we ventured over to the Mount of Olives. Rows upon rows of olive trees glistening under the stars first dipping into an escarpment then reemerging continuing up to the top. We noticed lanterns and torches along the hillside indicating there were other people making the same venture. As we started up the Mount, we passed a hedge and discovered the aroma of the sweet olive. This sugary smell made my mouth water. Sy even commented that it was like the candy store he remembered when he was a kid.

There were a few people but no crowds like we would be expecting. The narrow pathway up to the Mount was rocky. Trees lined the entire route making it a formidable place for one to hide out if needed. This would be an ideal place to stage an ambush or an abduction. Sy and Paul both agreed. This time, even more determined, we asked several people along the way if they know where Jesus is. Some ignored us and others just raised their shoulders and shook their heads. Others turned back towards us looking as if they are questioning the reason for us being there.

We looked at several other places at and around the Temple but still could not find Him. We had asked someone near the Temple and they quickly shook their head and walked away, straight to a Roman Guard. We watched as he was explaining to the guard and pointing in our direction. Our team quickly dissipated into the crowd.

Many people came for Passover, to hear Him and his sermons. But we could not find one person to tell us where he may be. We knew Jesus was going to the Last Supper the next evening. Or did we? Why has this task of locating one person been so elusive? I am starting to wonder if we are purposely being sent to the wrong locations time and time again. I am starting to wonder if the house we will be targeting tomorrow is indeed the place of the Last Supper.

After searching high and low we walked back to our quarters.

"Isn't it weird that no matter where we look, no matter who tells us where to go, we can't find Him?" Paul said rubbing his arms.

Sy chimed in, "All the missions we had been on all over the world, in remote areas, we had never had this problem locating one person. Captain, we may have another letdown tomorrow."

"Guys, right now we have no other choice but to wait. History may be our biggest enemy. What if, just what if, we can't change what has already happened? What if we could only observe?"

The room got silent. Thoughts raced inside each of our heads but no words were spoken. We sat there staring and listening to the crackle of the fire.

We decided, after an unsuccessful search, we would take our chances and we would let Jesus come to us.

* * *

Back at the Office, Jake Lepros was entranced in watching the movements on this mission. With the intermittent blips of green shown on the screen, emitting from the rings, Lepros had his doubts that the mission would be a success. The software development for this machine was not fine-tuned for tracking. Little did the team know, the equipment had its faults. It was incapable of tracking three different individuals going in separate directions in one city 2000 years in the past. Lepros was able only to see if the movement was east or west. The computer team was able to design a map of the city to overlay and superimpose the movements. It was not exact but it gave Lepros a piece of mind knowing the mission was active.

He constantly checked the monitors for any changes to the Bible and the team's locations. Totally consumed in this operation, Lepros had been unable to sleep or eat. Everything that needed to be in place for Lepros, was, except for this one minor detail: the final outcome, keeping Jesus from the Cross.

That is the part he needed and was miserably waiting for.

Lepros called in Sid and phoned Jimmy asking them both over and over if these guys, meaning the team, knew what they were doing.

"Are you sure these guys have all the tools they needed to get this job done?"

When Sid hurriedly arrived at Lepros' office, he reached into his back pocket and pulled out a handkerchief to wipe his brow.

"Yes, yes sir, I heard you, yes, they have everything they need," Sid said clearing his throat.

"I have Jimmy on the line," said Lepros.

"Hey Sid," Jimmy amusingly said through the speaker on the phone.

As Lepros' voice shook, and the perspiration covered his face, he said in a loud voice, "Are you sure these are the best? More than that...are you confident they will be successful?"

Lepros needed emotional support. He controlled many things, everything, but he couldn't control the outcome of this mission. Lepros' lifelong dreams of getting Him off the Cross were in the hands of three U.S. soldiers. "This is pathetic," he yelled as he slammed his fists onto his desk.

Jimmy, sounding a bit intoxicated, said he had to go and hung up the phone. This infuriated Lepros even more as he picked up the phone and threw it as far as it would travel.

Lepros lit up a cigarette, trying to find anything that could give him some peace of mind. The pressure was extraordinary! Sid stood there with his arms folded, biting his lower lip waiting for his boss to turn the hostilities towards him.

Lepros angrily discussed with Sid the meeting that the shareholders would be having in the next couple of days at the Office.

"I don't want any problems at this meeting!"

"We, we still have another day until the mission is complete," Sid cautiously replied.

Lepros knew that the meeting focused on what was about to transpire now, the changing of the Bible.

The upcoming meeting at the Office, would consist of people who have gone all in on the One World Order theory. Each partner or shareholder assumed that they will be in charge of one of the sections on the planet. Each also invested heavily in the Artificial Intelligence Project, known by some as the Christ Project. Lepros was trying to be positive and looking forward to bragging about the success of the mission. Lepros is also apprehensive if the mission fails, on what he needs to tell the partners.

* * *

In the middle of the night or very early morning, we heard a tap at the door, "Open up, it's me, Gabe."

Gabe entered and bestowed on us some fresh produce.

"It is admirable boys that you came all this way to Save Our Savior! The torture and vicious death He is about to undergo, is overwhelming."

He knows more than I gave him credit, I thought.

"Please, please I beg you, think about what you are planning to do. You may believe you are helping Christianity when in reality you are going to harm it."

I was still half asleep when he arrived and began preaching to us.

"Boys, Jesus died for us, for our sins, that is why he is called 'Savior'. Without the Crucifixion and Resurrection, our faith, mine and yours are in vain. Our faith is about the person of Jesus, that he is the Son of God and died for our sins. Our only obligation as his disciples is to try to live as he calls us to do, not rescue Him."

We looked at each other. Gabe had fire in his eyes that resonated from his heart. Inside, Gabe was resolute and delivered a strong message to us.

"Gabe, how do you know about the Crucifixion?"

"The Jews have been trying to silence Jesus for a while. They say he is blasphemous. The sentence for blasphemy is death."

Paul and Sy were very attentive at this point staring at Gabe waiting for his next words.

"Freeing Jesus from his death on the cross will leave a big hole in Christianity. Without Jesus giving up his life on the cross our future world would be impure and utter chaos. Secondly, there would be no Resurrection; if there is no death how can there be a Resurrection? Boys, your intentions are all well and good but not sound. We are not talking about a person; we are talking about the Lamb of God who takes away the sins of the world. This is not only about Jesus but also life after death, eternity. Please reconsider your mission. I offer no disrespect but, go back to where you came from."

We had this conversation days ago at the Office about whether it was right to save Jesus or not. We were given a much different explanation than Gabe had given us. We believed that the three of us could enhance Christianity. Sid had told us that if we could save Jesus from the Crucifixion, He would live a long life and do many more miracles. He would live a life that no one could argue the fact that he is the Son of God.

"Gabe, thank you for your input." I hesitantly stated to him.

Gabe studied the reaction on each of our faces. A solemn moment for us all.

The smoke from the fireplace backed up in the room a bit offering a pleasantly sweet aroma.

Gabe took a sip of water from the cup and left.

Paul asked, "How was it that Gabe stumbled onto us in the first place?"

"What about Jimmy?" I questioned, "How did Jimmy just appear in our lives?" said Sy.

All this was definitely getting into our heads; maybe it should be getting to our hearts instead. Maybe we should stop and listen to what our souls were telling us to do.

We had more questions, more thoughts, and more conflicting ideas about what we were here to do. Rescuing Jesus from death was what we were trained to do. Didn't others want to save him but couldn't or didn't? We three have the talent and capabilities to do it. Gabe assumed that Jesus would be persecuted for blasphemy, but how did Gabe know about the Resurrection?

Paul chimed in, "You know at different times in the Bible, there was divine intervention? Do you guys think that this may be one of those times with Gabe?"

"Man, sometimes he is a little creepy," said Sy.

"We need to go forward with our mission guys."

I was not very convincing. I could see each one, Paul and Sy thinking and trying to figure out what was the right thing to do here. Because we were trained to do and complete a mission, doesn't mean it was the right course. We have extracted people before and sometimes it was not in everyone's best interest. We need to sort this out. We need God to intercede to help us with our decision, or has He already?

Chapter 14

Holy Thursday

After Gabe left, we all became uneasy. His words were persistently recurrent. Each one of us tossed and turned. Yesterday was a tremendously unsettling day for us, both mentally and spiritually. Today would be no exception.

In Biblical terms, this is Holy Thursday.

When dawn finally appeared, we dressed and armed ourselves. We were fixed on finding Jesus and staying with him over the next two days. We had to determine the best opportunity to take Him and complete our mission. Once we located Jesus, He would not leave our sight until our job was completed. We would not leave Him until the ninth hour had passed and we were taken back to Nevada. *Mark 15:33 "And when the sixth hour had come, there was darkness over the whole land until the ninth hour."*

The first task of the day was to return to the original spot where we had arrived.

"Let's head out guys to where it all began."

We left our small enclave and spread out heading for the Golden Gate. In my mind, the thought kept recurring that just what if, accidentally one of us ran into Jesus now, while preparing for the final hours?

I had manipulated my mind to think about the worst-case

scenario; us being captured and not being able to fulfill our end of the deal.

Paul was the lead and gave Sy and me an all-clear after exiting the gate.

Sy looked relieved when we arrived at the spot. He had that secure appearance about him. I too felt comfortable here and safe.

"This place offers us the best cover," whispered Paul.

"I agree, we have looked around but I think this is still the safest location."

"Sy, our 'logistics guy', we need to find out how long it would take us to get Jesus over here. We need to determine that time, from three different possible extraction points."

"Yes, sir," Sy said mockingly.

"Ok, Paul, I would like you to go to the Mount of Olives. If we rescue Jesus there, how long will it take to get him here? Count one-one thousand, two-one thousand and so on. Do it going there and back to get the most accurate reading."

"Got it, sir."

"Sy, do the same thing from here to Golgotha, place of the skull, the place of the Crucifixion."

"Roger that, Cap."

"I will do similar measurements with the Cenacle."

"Boys, lets meet back at this location in approximately an hour," I said.

"Yes, sir, Cap."

"Yes, sir."

Paul looked dazed and somewhat confused. He said, "Captain, when the final hour passes, will we be returned from this spot, right here?"

He was taking deep exaggerated breaths.

"Paul, as long as we have our rings on, we will be returned from anywhere."

He shook his head and closed his eyes; I could see the relief in his demeanor.

"This is where we will bring Jesus and keep Him safe until the final hour has passed."

"What about the apostles?" exclaimed Sy.

"If the situation arises, we could take a few of the apostles. They will be skittish once Jesus is arrested so I don't believe any of them will be sticking around knowing they could be next."

"Chicken shits!" Sy said under his breath.

"Here, we would be able to administer aid to Jesus, without the risk of being found. We would stay here until the Friday deadline has passed. At that time, when we are transported back, we will know that the mission had been a success.

Lingering in the back of my mind is the thought of being able to abort this mission at any time. This decision belonged to us solely. We only have to push one button to go back and reanalyze this whole thing. To my team, aborting the mission is a sign of failure, but this team does not do failure, period. The thought of being able to perform 'do-overs' until we got it right was intriguing, however it was never discussed in training. It made me wonder why it was not talked about? Another red flag and the hair on the back of my neck began to rise at the thought of it.

"Guys, if we decide to abort this job, and return back, Lepros would be able reanalyze this mission if we supplied him with enough important information; like how many guards are around and the conditions of the surrounding area of the last supper and Mount of Olives. We could do it, one more time."

"Sid supposedly did a test run before us. Surely, he observed all the potential hot spots and based our training on those issues, didn't he?" asked Paul.

I thought about it but failed to come up with some logical answers; the numbers were not adding up.

"Did Lepros consult with religious authorities before he decided to undertake this endeavor? He did, didn't he?"

We both stared at Sy.

"Was this mission too secret for Lepros to even mention this to anyone outside his corporation?" asked Sy.

I probably should have asked those questions during training. With more information, gathered from us, we could go back and forth in time and we could get this right!

Little did we know Lepros had only one plan, one shot at this and it was our job to live up to our agreement.

Chapter 15

Search for the Target

We returned from our time trials and determined that Golgotha was the farthest at about twenty-three minutes. Mount of Olives was only twelve and the Cenacle was only ten, the last two under cover of darkness.

"Guys, if we take Jesus from the Crucifixion, we need to transport Him in a cart. We can't be running down the road carrying a body, it would draw too much attention."

"I'll say," blurted Paul.

"We need to get a wheeled cart, a rickshaw, and leave it in the general area of Golgotha prior to the Crucifixion. When we extract Jesus, we would place Him in the cart, cover Him, and walk back here."

"I will get on that cart."

"Thanks Paul."

"Also, there was darkness in the sixth hour to the ninth hour, but if we take Jesus before Him being nailed to the cross, I don't know if we will have that darkness for our cover; better make sure we have a lantern in that cart, just in case."

"Will do Captain."

We were still anxious and set out again to look for the elusive, Jesus. Sy enlisted the help of Alexander and Rufas. The boys seemed more interested in the merchandise the vendors were selling than finding Jesus, it frustrated Sy. There were fountains in the city where many gathered that Sy checked out, but no luck. Sy searched the Temple area and around the southern steps to no avail.

Paul thought pretty logically and checked the countryside outside the city where larger groups might be able to assemble. He walked across the Kidron Valley to the Garden of Gethsemane located on the Mount of Olives. Paul sat there for a short time admiring the City of David from that vantage point wondering where Jesus may be. Still no sight of Him. We wanted to see Him and listen to Him.

I was just thinking about Gabe when BAM! We come face to face, each turning a blind corner from different directions.

My blood started to boil! "Where's Jesus!" I interrogated as if I knew he was keeping that information from us.

"Well, my guess is as good as yours, Captain."

Trying to calm myself down, "I know you are trying to protect Him, but we are not here to hurt him."

Gabe raised his hands defensively.

"You will meet Jesus soon. But I must warn you, He too has a mission."

Gabe quickly walked away before I could even digest what he had just said.

Up until now, we have been unsuccessful. It was unusual for us to go out to locate someone and be thwarted each time, and at each location. We had either just missed Him or He hadn't been there. It was frustrating for us. I was holding the thought in my heart of what Gabe had just told me; 'you will meet Jesus soon.'

The morning came and went and the afternoon was racing right behind it. Whenever I couldn't get a grip on something like 'how fast the morning flew by', I questioned the way I felt, blaming it on time travel. Somehow, in my mind, I have this inability to focus, at times. Sometimes I freeze for a few moments and can't move. We still did not understand just how our bodies were affected by being thrown back in time. Are we missing or could we be missing some key body parts, like brain cells? Were we entirely and completely transported? Why do I, at times, feel unable to perform my leadership role? Why am I feeling inept and incapable of performing my duties?

Are there other forces at work besides time travel?

Chapter 16

Dinner and the Mount

It was getting to be that time. The sun was beginning to set. We all decided that we should locate strategic spots for us to observe the two-story building where Jesus and the apostles would meet this evening. With our garb and weapons, we headed to the location of the Last Supper.

Just the thought of being that close to Jesus overwhelmed me. I kept looking down at my hands, over and over like I was expecting them to disappear at any moment. I didn't feel right. Every inch of my body trembled uncontrollably while I was thinking about meeting Jesus. I was constantly adjusting my clothing trying to get comfortable and was not succeeding. I have never experienced this, ever! We were so close now.

We originally questioned the validity of this being the location of the Last Supper. Paul and Sy had located two other two-story houses and watched them for a while. As sunset approached, the other two homes showed very little activity. Paul and Sy returned.

"Cap, I think this is the right place."

"I agree Paul. People have been gathering here like a whirlwind for the last hour."

We found a couple of spots around the building that looked strategic enough to observe all entrances and sides of the building.

"Cap, I will take the north and northwest side of the building."

"Thanks, Sy."

"Paul, take the front with me. Take that corner over there." I motioned.

We each took our places. The locations we picked offered the complete view of each side of the building. Every doorway, every opening, was in clear view. Our locations did not appear out of place. There were many other people who also wanted to see Jesus and they too gathered around this house where He would entertain the apostles this evening. We got comfortable and waited. Time passed seemingly ever so slowly.

As the sun set and the darkness began to creep in on us, we saw several people enter the building on the side entrance. I assumed that maybe the worker bees or some family that owned the building were coming in at that time. They were carrying baskets of what I assumed was food. Others entering the building were carrying jugs of either wine or water. None of them used the front entrance.

We had no idea what the apostles or even Jesus actually looked like. During training, we looked at several paintings and read descriptions but nothing was definite. Sid had told us that he went back in time to Jerusalem and saw Jesus, but thinking about that, he never gave us a clear description of Him.

Moments passed and I observed another group of men who were conversing as they walked slowly toward the building. I determined that from my vantage point, they were headed in my direction. Other people around me also took notice, stood, and began to cheer. Some in the crowd knelt. Others, young and old, stared at the group as they made their way through the crowds and moved closer to the house. Others shouted, "Jesus,

Jesus!"

As this group edged closer, I could feel their presence descending upon me. It was getting hard for me to breathe. There was some type of aura surrounding them, an almost mystical radiance. I began wringing my hands together. My mouth felt dry. The crowd felt their presence also. The excitement was in the air. Reality struck me, I was afraid! I was terrified! My heart was going to beat out of my chest!

I looked over and saw Paul who was now standing, and he signaled for Sy to come his way to join him and watch as this group edged closer.

One of the men, the tallest in the group, was being somewhat shielded by the others.

"Yeshua, Yeshua," the crowd shouted. "Rabbi," shouted others.

The nearer they got, the clearer it was that He was special. There was an exaltation, a glow so indescribable surrounding this entire group. It appeared to be Him! It was like I had seen His face before! Sometime in my life, I know I have seen His face, possibly several times in my life. As He and the group started to pass me, He paused for a brief moment, stopped, turned, and looked at me and I at Him. His face was radiant and gleaming. He smiled at me and then continued walking. Peace came over my entire existence!

It was Jesus. He looked at me! What did his smile to me mean? Did he know why I was there? Of course, he did! The only way I can describe what just happened is I felt that my being had completely changed. I had loved Jesus and God through faith before; now I can say I have seen Him, I am a true believer.

John 20:29 "Because you have seen Me, do you now

believe? Blessed are they who did not see and yet believed."

This group of men numbering about twelve and Jesus began to enter the building. Others, men and women were anxiously waiting at the doorway for Jesus. They greeted Jesus at the entrance with hugs. After the group of men had entered, the others followed.

I went over to Sy and Paul and shared what I had just experienced. I shared with them the smile and we tried to analyze it. I felt the presence of the Holy Spirit through my entire body. Jesus knew who I was and what I was doing there. My question was, "Is He pleased that we are going to save him or not? What was that smile telling me?"

"You are a Blessed man!" said Paul.

"Blessed from the Highest!" said Sy.

"This is it, guys, the Last Supper."

Paul looked out over the crowd that had gathered.

"It's so surreal to me. This whole mission. Vegas, time travel, Jerusalem, Jesus."

"It's not about what's written in the Bible or other accounts anymore; we are living proof. We saw! We were told that when we return, our memories will revert to when we left and all this will be forgotten."

"How did Sid remember?" asked Sy, bringing us back to reality with that remark.

We paused and contemplated the question. After we mentally regrouped, our attention was refocused on the rescue.

"The apostles, are not even aware that this is the Last Supper. I don't think that Judas even thought that Jesus would be crucified because of what he was about to do," said Paul.

"Only us and Jesus know."

As the celebration continued inside, and with us on the

outside, we could hear distant music in the background coming from the city. There were crickets chirping, the sky was clear, and a chill after the sunset had taken a grip. There was a crescent moon hanging overhead, and we sat together and waited.

Paul broke the silence.

"When I was a teen, a neighbor invited my foster family to a Passover dinner. They called it the Seder. It was a ritual retelling the story of the Israelites liberation from slavery. They used to read from a book called the Haggadah while the meal was served. The book explained the foods on the seder plate and their association with Passover. The book recounts the highlights of the Exodus and included songs, prayers, questions, and vignettes."

"Quite interesting," said Sy.

"It was a lot of fun."

"Do you think they are doing that right now upstairs?"

"Possibly, but from reading different books, such as the Bible, it appears to have been a solemn celebration, at least for Jesus."

"Jesus knows what's coming, but I don't believe the apostles are on the same page," replied Sy.

An hour or so passed, and as anticipated, one of the guests who entered the two-story with Jesus, darted from the building and headed to the city running at what appeared to be full thrust.

"That would be Judas Iscariot." I whispered.

We discussed earlier about taking Judas out and not letting him report to the authorities which was one of the scenarios that we had played out during training. It was all in motion now. I had thought about taking Judas out right then and there but something inside told me not to; to wait. Besides, there were hundreds of people around.

"Paul, follow him."

Sid had suggested during training, we let as much of this play out as we could as not to alter too much of what the Bible says. Sid explicitly said that we should allow Christ to go to trial, be convicted and sentenced, and continue to the Crucifixion. Sid had explained, at that point, that there would still be God but no Son of God or Resurrection which would be totally in line with the Old Testament. At least not at this time.

I questioned his motives then, and now, as we watch Judas leave our sight, I question them again. What did Sid want us to do? Was he expecting us to die along with Jesus? This would have been the perfect time to stop the Crucifixion. We could have stopped Judas, and killed him, and it would be done. Judas would go on and kill himself anyway. We didn't need to be delicate about anything. Sid had been quite adamant about waiting.

I kept pondering the look and the smile Jesus had given me.

I was led to believe earlier in my life that just Jesus and the apostles came from dinner and wandered alone up to the Mount of Olives, but that was not so, I was soon to discover. They and hundreds of followers and admirers went to the Mount. Those followers were also hanging out as we were, to get a glimpse of Jesus and to hear Him speak. It was a festive time that's why it is referred to as the 'Festival of Freedom.' The three of us, even though we too were admirers, were there for different reasons than the rest of the crowd.

Soon, Jesus reappeared and headed out. We followed Him and the apostles along with all the other believers and worshipers down the road and to the Mount of Olives. We all were on the move. It was a sea of lanterns and torches swaying back and forth moving in one direction. It was as if we were all following a movie star who walked through the door, all trying to get a glimpse or a brief conversation. It was the sheep following our Shepherd.

Paul had just returned and said that Judas had entered a building: but he himself was unable to go inside with him. Paul kept blowing out a series of short breaths then a deep breath in, repeatedly.

"Are you ok?"

"Yeah, fine. Just feel a little out of it sometimes."

"I have been getting like that, too, Captain," said Sy. "Do you think time travel has something to do with that?"

"It's all new to me also boys so I can't answer that."

Paul and Sy seemed a bit anxious, a little out of character for both of them but under these circumstances, understandable.

Both were always, matter-of-fact guys, with nothing but the planned mission on their minds. This was not the case here. We were talking Jesus! The Only Begotten Son of God! I, on the other hand, am guilty of all the above, however, I am the captain, the leader. I am becoming a follower here when I should be focusing on leading and bringing Jesus to safety.

The quivering in my body began again, noticeably. Paul and Sy looked at me.

"What's happening?" said Sy.

"I don't know........... I am ok, come on, let's move."

I returned to normal.

I am still the one who will decide just when this operation goes into full motion and when this thing is a go. All this feels so unnatural, dreamlike and to think that I, we, my team, my friends, my brothers, have been chosen for this event; this event that changes history from here on out, forever.

As we hiked up the Mount, I saw one of the apostles gesture for Jesus to follow him to a more secluded area, as we know it, Gethsemane. I signaled for Sy and Paul to spread out further, to be able to do surveillance on the Mount. We watched as Jesus followed his apostles. Jesus, who now is a distance from us, turned to some of his apostles and spoke to the small group. Three of the men from the small group stepped forward to go with Jesus. The other apostles stayed behind keeping the crowd that had gathered, back.

Jesus went with the three he had selected and went a little further up the hill. Following, my team maneuvered a bit closer and saw Jesus talking to the three. When that conversation ended Jesus walked away from them even further up, to a secluded area by himself, and knelt.

We moved within earshot and watched as Jesus prayed for a long time. We were close enough to see Him expel His breath in the chilled air. From the light of the torch that surrounded him, we were close enough to see the sweat on His face and steam rising from his body while he was in the kneeling position. His sweat appeared dark. It shimmered as it crept down on his face.

Luke 22:44 "and being in agony, He prayed more earnestly. Then His sweat became like great drops of blood falling to the ground."

Medical science has found that in extreme cases of anxiety, a rare condition can occur called *hematidrosis*, sweat that contains blood or blood pigments. I had seen this during my military service on the battlefield in severe injury cases. A sad moment for us as this part of the Holy Bible has come to life. The other three who Jesus had brought with Him had laid down nearby on some rocks and were motionless.

We sat and watched, as time passed.

Jesus turned, stood and walked over to the three who had fallen asleep. He stared at them and became visibly upset shouting at them. One of the three got up off the ground, grabbed Jesus' hand, and started to say something to Jesus; that seemed to settle Jesus down. He and the three then sat and talked.

Jesus got to His feet, said a few things to the three then sat, then stood again. He appeared agitated. Each time he stood, he paced before he sat. He was dramatically using his hands each time he spoke. Jesus kept looking around and at times looked in our direction. We were hidden in the brush and blended in just so we wouldn't be conspicuous.

It was getting closer to the time.

We heard some type of disturbance a little further down the hill and noticed a cluster of light, then fire moving through the olive trees. It looked and sounded like a crowd of people were coming closer and about to invade the space Jesus had created for himself. The people who had been approaching seemed to spread out as they got nearer. It was as if someone was pushing them all from the middle outward, causing them either to move right or to move left.

The first to emerge from the middle were the servants of the Pharisees. Then, lo and behold, the man we saw earlier running from the house, was Judas. He frantically stormed up the side of the steep slope outpacing the Roman soldiers, the High Priest, and the Pharisees who had been following him. From our vantage point, we could see Judas run up to Jesus and say a couple of words then he kissed Jesus

"There He is!" Shouted someone from the recently arrived

mob.

The three of us moved in even closer. We had to determine if this was the time we would get Jesus out of here.

"Not now, stand down."

We just missed our chance. When Jesus walked over to pray, that would have been the time to take him. What were we thinking? Were we captivated by the moment, mesmerized? Maybe there are other forces, not the ones we can see, that are keeping us back.

Looking at the large crowd and the scores of guards that had just arrived, we determined that now, was a no-go. We had no doubt we could still get the job done but with a crowd that size, there would be too many casualties and that was what we were trying to avoid. Consciously or subconsciously, we missed that narrow window of opportunity, I missed it.

There was fighting in the middle and small groups had engaged all around. Some of the followers appeared to be standing up to the guards. We saw someone, one of the apostles, with a sword, raise the sword then strike one of the servants with it. From our vantage point, we saw Jesus move in quickly bend down, and pick something up from the ground. Jesus then placed that item on the side of the servant's head. The Bible said that Jesus had bent down and recovered the ear from the ground and held it to the side of his head, the man had healed and then he believed.

Jesus then shouted, "Stop!"

The fighting stopped instantly. You could hear a pin drop it was so quiet. The servant who had his ear returned to his head, reeled back and knelt. Other people around, even some guards, dropped their weapons and fell to their knees. Everyone who witnessed knew they were in the presence of Holiness. It was a solemn moment. All who saw what Jesus had just done, believed at that moment, that He was who He said He was. My team was right in the middle and witnessing the Greatest Story ever told as it was occurring. The disciples of Jesus, seeing that they were outnumbered, dropped their weapons, slumped their shoulders, and turned to walk away.

It appeared that most knew what was coming next.

Jesus stood still, silence had covered the Mount, He looked around, then proclaimed, "Let's go."

The soldiers, High Priest and Pharisees with their servants, and of course, Judas, had come to arrest and deliver Jesus for trial. They bound Jesus' extended hands and they proceeded back down the Mount and back into the city where Jesus would soon face the trial and the people He came to save. The believers and followers who were there watching this enfold, began to scatter for fear of retaliation from the Roman Empire.

The three of us split up as planned following Jesus from a distance. Our options for taking Jesus were now getting limited. I as the leader, had blown the best chance to save Jesus. I am now, doubting myself and this mission we agreed to take on.

We have the trials which would be the most dangerous option left, followed by Jesus carrying the cross then lastly, just before the Crucifixion. My only saving grace mentally, is that Sid suggested we take Jesus as close to the Crucifixion as possible. If I kept thinking what Sid wanted, then we hadn't wasted any opportunities.

Paul, Sy, and I met up again just outside the Sanhedrin Council building where approximately seventy-one members would be assembled for the first trial. Annas is the former high priest; Caiaphas is the current high priest. Here, Jesus will be charged with blasphemy, claiming to be the Son of God.

Sid had told us that the Jewish leaders hated Jesus so much that they broke their own laws to prosecute Him. There were supposed to be no trials during feast times; each member of the court was to vote individually, but on this night, they convicted Jesus by acclamation. If a death penalty was given, a night must pass before the sentence was carried out. The Jews had no authority to execute anyone. No trial was to be held at night. The accused was to receive counsel. No incriminating questions were to be asked of the accused. This proceeding was an act of pure hatred.

There was a small window of opportunity after the trial by the Jews. Jesus would be taken over to Pilate after he was beaten. Different charges would be brought against Jesus such as inciting a riot, forbidding the people to pay their taxes, and claiming to be a King.

"There is so much security around Jesus right now."

"This is not a good time," said Sy.

"Pilate's next move will be to send Jesus to Herod because it's his jurisdiction and Pilate found no reason to kill Jesus."

"These buildings are so close to one another. We will only get a glimpse of Jesus as he passes from one place to another," Paul said.

In Herod's quarters, Herod did not get the answers he wanted from Jesus so he ridiculed Jesus and sent Him back to Pilate.

"Pilate will try to appease the Jews by having Jesus scourged but the Jews will want more. Scourging is the type of torture, a whipping, designed to tear flesh from the back of the one being punished."

"I would like to prevent that if we could," said Paul.

"Pilate will make his best effort to have Jesus released by offering Barabbas in exchange for Jesus. We can get in the public viewing area of the Praetorium, where this trial will be heard."

"Most of the guards plus Pontius Pilate will be at the trial. That would not be in anyone's best interest if we attempted it then," said Sy.

"There would be casualties and it will be a threat to our own safety," exclaimed Paul.

"This extraction must occur when we have the advantage."

We did not have much time left. This mission was unique because of who our target was. We could not do this in the wee hours of the night because the Crucifixion was going to take place in just a few hours. We had no cover from either night or weather.

As we entered the open-air staging area for the trial, a man, staggering and possibly not in his right mind came up to us as we were about to split up. Wide-eyed, saliva dripping from his mouth, his hair and clothing in disarray, this person, looking directly at each one of us uttered, "Think not how man thinks, think as God thinks."

He turned and quickly scrambled away as fast as he had entered our space. The messenger got our attention all right; then he delivered a message. Paul and Sy immediately looked at me as if I were to break down and analyze what was just conveyed to us.

"Take your posts, guys."

The message we heard did not completely resonate with us right away. Like a dull pain, that message became bigger and bigger in each of us as the day proceeded. We waited for the moment we could see Jesus again.

As we took positions for the final trial of Jesus, our hearts were torn between saving Jesus and ultimately, letting Jesus save us. Are we to save Jesus? Or, are we going to stand by as observers, waiting for him to be tortured, as the others did, then watch him be put to death to save mankind?

Surely, if we save Jesus, God would find another way to forgive our sins, I argued to myself. But who are we to put that on God? Who are we to intrude on God's plan? Our will is not stronger than God's will. We are thinking as man thinks, not as God thinks.

From a great distance in time, 2000 years later, a person can sit back in his chair and Monday morning quarterback, and say ok, if we were in Jerusalem with Jesus, we could have done this or we could have done that. But actually, to be here, in the now, it's a much different story.

Silently under my breath, I prayed, "Father, forgive us for what we are about to do. If it is your will, so be it."

We blended in with the crowd trying not to be conspicuous, when lo and behold I saw Gabe talking to Paul. Then, I saw Paul shaking his head as Gabe turned to leave.

While I was watching Paul and Gabe, a woman chasing a child, ran into me. She looked at me. I was expecting 'a sorry' or 'excuse me,' but instead she said, "Leave this be and return home."

She continued to walk away, melting into the crowd never to be seen by me again.

Paul worked his way over to me and said that Gabe, again, told him that we had been sent here by Lepros for the wrong reasons and that it has been written that Jesus will die on the cross for our sins and that God wants it that way.

"Did Gabe say Lepros?"

"Yes, by name."

"How does Gabe know about Lepros?"

"Don't know, just passing on the message."

Sy had worked his way over to us also. He said that while he was standing and observing near an opening to the courtyard, he heard a voice say, "Jesus is King, this is God's will not your will, Sy".

"Captain, I looked around, I didn't see anyone talking to me."

"Let this all play out, guys. We will all know when it's the right time."

We all had received messages not to rescue Jesus. Our minds told us we were on a mission, our souls were telling us differently.

Since we had arrived in Jerusalem, there has been constant conflict between spirit and body - whether we should complete our mission or just stay on the sidelines. Being here in person, actually living and seeing the works of God, and knowing the purpose for His actions, helps us understand the significance of the Crucifixion.

I know that we agreed to all the reasoning we discussed in training, however, the signs since we have been here, indicated just the opposite. There is a message from man, then there is a message from God. Who would be pleased if we succeeded in this mission? Who would be pleased if we didn't?

In the end, I don't have to face other people and give an account of my life; in the end, I stand before God.

Chapter 17

Good Friday - Crucifixion

A couple of hours have passed and it is becoming daylight as we wait with the crowd in the open piazza, We are waiting for the trial to begin. Word has it that is the place where Jesus will be tried in public. The crowd I would say was a bit uneasy, tense.

It was early in the morning and those who had gathered displayed an uncontrollable energy, rocking, talking, and frantically moving their hands in all directions. This was no ordinary trial. In the cast of people eagerly waiting for it to begin, emotions ran high.

Some women were crying consoling each other; there were even men bothered emotionally and you could tell by the anger on their faces as they ranted and raved at anyone nearby who would listen. Then there were others acting nonchalantly and seemingly enjoying the moment. We noticed a few of the apostles along the outer wall, who were trying to hide their faces for fear of being recognized as associates of Jesus. They were spread out in the crowd.

It was somber for us because we knew what was ahead. These people did not know that this was one of the most profound moments ever experienced by mankind. Unknowingly, every one of them was a part of the abomination that was about to take place. The three of us are now also witnesses of it.

As Christians and as soldiers, we are in a position to do something about this. We have the tools necessary to complete the job.

We were angry that no one here lifted a hand to help Jesus and to save Him. We were here, Paul, Sy, and I to do just that. This mission is so conflicting that it is hindering all that we do. One moment we are a go then the next; our consciences tell us to stand down. Would we lay our lives on the line for Jesus? Absolutely, if that were God's wishes. We needed to act soon if this was going to be the case. Time was running out.

Anticipation stirred as Roman soldiers stood along the stage. I heard a rooster crowing and immediately looked towards one of the apostles who was standing nearby. A guard had just walked up and said something to him. He shook his head while covering his face, turned, and walked away. It was him, Peter. I had witnessed his denial of Jesus Christ.

I had seen Judas earlier but I did not see him now. I am assuming that his guilt is keeping him away from here and the other apostles. But then again, he's a coward. Judas is most likely hiding in a corner, observing this trial.

A man appeared center stage and was recognized by the crowd. He distinguished himself by wearing a white tunic with a length just below his knees. He extended his right arm out as if he was greeting the crowd before him. He had a large gold-breasted plate on his chest and a bright red sash draped from his right shoulder to his hip. He reminded me of our military general who was about to give a speech in front of a graduating class, dressed in his finest.

He appeared large on the stage. This was Pontius Pilate. He held a massive sword in his left hand, blade towards the ground.

His hands were huge and rugged-looking as he held the handle firmly.

We were almost at the tail end of the crowd, spread out in the back near the apostles. We couldn't hear all that was said but from knowing the Bible, we realized what was taking place. At that moment, more guards appeared, and Jesus was in the middle of them. He was blindfolded and appeared to have been savagely beaten. His face was swollen on the left side. There was blood from the side of his head down along his neck to his shoulders. His long hair was also blotched with blood and some patches were missing. The clothes Jesus had on were not torn nor did they have blood on them. The guards must have changed Jesus' clothes prior to bringing him out. I tapped my heart three times. I pray to God in Heaven to help us do His will, whatever His will may be!

Supposedly, when we return back to the future, we will not remember any of this. But my heart is full of the Grace of Our Lord. No one, I mean no one can wipe that away from my heart and soul. As for my mind, I will do everything in my power to never forget.

This was Jesus Christ Our Savior right in front of us! I stood and stared in amazement. The crowd was in an uproar of mixed emotions that Jesus was there shouting, "Jesus, Jesus", yet, when Pilate began to speak, they quieted right down, not wanting to miss a word as the trial began. I know from the gospels how the apostles were able to quote Pilate and remember everything that happened right here because it was so surreal. I now understand that.

A woman wearing a golden tunic with a white sash and gold shoes and a white and golden veil, dashed onto the stage and had a short emotional conversation with Pilate. When the conversation with Pilate had ended, she put both her hands to her face, her body shuttered, and her shoulder drooped as she left the stage visibly upset. This lady was Claudia Procula, the wife or girlfriend of Pontus Pilate. She was also a believer in Jesus and who he was. We know from writings that Claudia had a dream that the Roman Empire would be condemned if Jesus were harmed. Claudia had just shared that dream with Pilate and asked him to have nothing to do with the trial of Jesus, but she was summarily dismissed.

Pilate moved closer to Jesus and had his blindfold removed.

"Are you the King of the Jews?"

Jesus replied, "Yes, it is as you say."

"Don't you hear the testimony they are bringing against you?"

Jesus did not reply.

Pilate announced several times that Jesus was an innocent man and had committed no crimes against the Roman Empire.

"Jesus is from Galilee and he must be sent to Herod who has the authority over him."

The crowd reacted in the same disgruntled way by shouting and making vulgar sounds. Jesus, with no expression on his face, was forcibly taken away again by the guards.

Paul, Sy, and I left the courtyard and followed Jesus to Herod's Place which was just a block away. We watched as Jesus was pushed into the building.

Taking a position outside, Sy exclaimed, "Captain, this is not a good time to take Jesus."

"Let's think this through. Our best chance now is to wait up until the actual Crucifixion. There will be fewer guards and fewer people. We trained for that; let's execute then."

"None of us want to see this happening to Jesus, but our goal is to save him from death on the cross. I agree, let's wait," Paul interjected.

"Guys, let's just stay close for now. I don't need any
of us to be separated at this time."

About an hour later, Jesus, escorted by the guards, was returned from Herod's place. He again took center stage, this time with a known criminal. We followed him back to the courtyard. We moved closer to the stage in front. I heard comments from people around us, who knew of this criminal, that this guy was bad, and his name was Barabbas. The crowd reacted to the criminal by yelling and booing at him. The guards were amused at the crowd's reaction.

I could tell from the way Pilate viewed the crowd that he was measuring its mood and assessing how to proceed for his political advantage. As we know, he would eventually succumb to pressure from some of the crowd. The chief priests and the elders of the people that had gathered, needed to have Jesus put to death. They could no longer have Jesus, work miracles and wonders because it threatened their authoritative position in a religious society that they dominated. There was no room for Jesus in their world. They held the power to control the Jews for the Roman Empire. Pilate knew that and gave in to them.

It was customary before the feast of Passover, that the Roman governor granted clemency to one criminal as an act of goodwill towards the Jews whom he governed. Pilate picked the worst of the worst versus the teacher and miracle worker.

Pilate had picked out this prisoner, Barabbas, a murderer, and wanted to let the crowd choose between the two; who in fact gets released. Pilate knew how bad this dude was. He had hoped that the people would think about the fact that Barabbas would be free to ravage the citizens again and would come to realize that Jesus would be the best choice to be released. Pilate was hoping by doing this he would be able to set Jesus free with only the flogging. The crowd initially started to chant for Jesus to be released but the Jews, the higher echelon anyway, had the upper hand and louder voices and demanded Barabbas be released.

By this time Pilate was beside himself. He looked uncomfortable on stage. He was sweating and paced back and forth.

"Which of the two do you want me to release to you?" asked the governor in a loud but shaky voice.

"Barabbas," the crowd answered.

"What shall I do then with Jesus who is called Christ?"

"Crucify Him!"

"Why, what crimes has he committed?"

"Crucify Him!"

Pilate pleaded with the crowd, "Crucify your King?"

Those near me wept openly when hearing those words; some turned away and left. Pilate appeared to be surprised and stated again to the crowd, "that the charges against Jesus were baseless." He asked the crowd three times. The Jews in the crowd became louder and demanded Jesus be crucified. The voices were clearer from the front.

Someone yelled, "If you let this man Jesus go, you are no friend of Caesar." Pilate who had this authority was afraid of losing it, and gave in to the mob.

Pilate saw he was getting nowhere. He took water and in front of everyone, washed his hands.

"I am innocent of this man's blood. It is now your responsibility."

Jesus would bear the punishment of Barabbas who most

likely deserved it. Jesus would also be convicted and bear our sins! Pilate at that moment ordered Jesus stripped of his now white robe and scourged in front of the crowd.

I turned away remembering the time I had wandered into the kitchen and spotted a quarter on the kitchen counter. I grabbed the quarter and placed it in my pocket. As I headed towards the door, the house mom appeared, with fire in her eyes, holding a belt in her hand. She began wailing on me ever so endlessly. Striking me over and over again. I begged for her to stop. The pain was so distressing. I noticed the blood on my hands that had come from the punishment. This was nothing compared to what we were about to witness. I am in control of that belt now. In my mind, I can't let that happen to Jesus.

We saw Pilate speak with Jesus and watched as Pilate became visibly upset, bent his shoulders then rose up. Pilate quickly turned and yelled out, "Behold the man."

We knew what came next and we prepared ourselves. Pilate yelled out again, "His blood be upon us and our children." Pilate released Barabbas and handed Jesus over to be scourged.

Pilate and the High Priest who was close by, stared at each other when the verdict was announced, "Crucify Him!"

The High Priest arrogantly nodded his satisfaction over the outcome. In the High Priest's eyes, Jesus was a blasphemer! More than that, He was in their way.

'It's just like the Last Supper when Judas ran from the building to alert the authorities of Jesus' whereabouts. There he was again, I recognized him, running from this courtyard.'

The weeping for Jesus intensified. The crowd, the supporters of Jesus, became visibly angry. "Coward! Coward!" shouted some in the crowd. "Death to Ceasar, death to Pilate," shouted others. There was some pushing and shoving of the high priests before they left the courtyard.

The guards came out of the building and onto the stage laughing at all the ruckus that had been going on and placed an object on the head of Jesus. Jesus winched in pain as the crown of thorns was forced onto his head.

"King of the Jews," scoffed the guard.

The blood immediately ran from the top of his head down onto his face. Jesus was taken out of the court.

I watched as Paul worked his way to the front near the stage area. There was no reason or plan that Paul should be anywhere near the stage. I motioned for Sy to move in because I was not sure what Paul was going to do. Paul had that look on his face, determination, anger. He had not notified me or Sy and I know how emotional this was for us and that possibly Paul might take some action on his own. I didn't want him to do anything without us being a part of that decision.

Navigating through an irritated crowd, was not easy. Some people had pushed back as I attempted to get around them; others called me gentile, in a derogatory way. I managed to work my way closer to Paul, who was now in front next to the stage area. One of the guards who had been berating Jesus, the one who had placed the crown on Jesus' head, was walking down a couple of stairs near Paul. He turned nonchalantly toward the guard and brushed against him. The guard tumbled down the stairs.

No one in the crowd saw this as all eyes were focused on Jesus as he was being led away.

As I approached Paul he said to me, "I couldn't take it anymore."

I looked down at the guard. The guard was still out on the ground, his eyes rolled back and he was twitching. A couple of other guards also leaving the stage, just walked over to the guard on the ground laughing at him, not knowing just what had taken place.

Paul had tazed the guard!

"Let's get out of here," I said to Paul.

I noticed that Sy had stopped going forward when I reached Paul knowing I was there with him. Sy motioned to us that he was going to the exit. We were not getting Jesus out now. We would all be caught and crucified if we tried it here. It took some time for Paul and me to snake back through the crowd which was still quite heated over the decision to release Barabbas. By the comments I was hearing, it seems to me they were more upset over Barabbas being released to the community than Jesus being crucified.

After leaving the trial, we went to the road where we knew Jesus would be walking with the cross, Via Dolorosa. The street was narrow and dusty. It follows along the outer wall of the city. It's on an incline which makes it difficult to walk on let alone carry a cross. Via Dolorosa is a winding road that goes uphill for several blocks until it reaches the first set of gates to the city. Along the route we found a place along the side that gave us the best vantage point.

We stood there solemnly awaiting, along with hundreds of others, the fate of our Savior and feeling a sense of regret, knowing we could have taken out most if not all the guards, and taken Jesus. Then again, our souls kept telling us this wasn't a wise idea. The will of God seemed to be much greater than any weapon or force and it was getting stronger the closer we got to the Crucifixion.

We waited outside with a clear view of the building where we knew Jesus would soon appear. We talked briefly about the rescue and said that we would wait until the time of the actual Crucifixion. I wanted to take out as many of the Roman guards as possible. However, like any mission, there is only one focus and we couldn't lose sight of the object of our mission. We needed to keep our personal opinions and feelings tucked deep inside, especially for this mission.

Our best plan of action, the only plan left, centered on waiting until Jesus arrived at the place of the Skull. The guards would be minimal there, and the crowd much smaller. We could free Jesus, tend to his injuries, and get him out of the city. If we are injured even severely, we would be returned home shortly after, to receive medical assistance since we would be on track for the scheduled time to be returned. We also had our mission accomplished alerts on hand to whisk us all back to where we came from if it deemed necessary or that we completed the mission sooner. We were still confident that we could pull off this mission.

* * *

Lepros, back at the desert office in Nevada, kept staring at the clock, the GPS, and the overhead that read JOHN 19:30. There were intermittent signals on the GPS that seemed to rattle Lepros totally. Every time we were not where Lepros thought we should be as indicated by the GPS, he erupted with anger, pounding his fists, making harsh comments about the team, and belittling anyone who was near. The break point was edging closer.

"Surely they can take him out at any moment now," Lepros shouted.

* * *

The street was lined with people. The final decision and

preparations had been made regarding the Crucifixion, and we were waiting for the march to begin.

"This guys, is the stations of the cross in real time," I said to them as we split up.

Again, the three of us were at a distance just far enough so that we were in each other's sight. The procession began what I guessed to be around 8-8:30. Whatever anyone's position was, all eyes would be fixed on Jesus.

It was kind of like a mix of a funeral procession and a parade. Men and women were weeping, some uncontrollably; guards on foot and on horses all had whips or as they called them *flagrums*; and there were rabble-rousers, laughing and antagonizing the crowd up and down the street.

"Oh, poor Jesus, Boo Hoo," one man kept repeating rubbing his fists in his eyes in a mocking gesture, as he went down the street to different people in attendance. The heat of the day intensified. There were no clouds in the sky. The air was dry. It was as if the world around us had stopped and everything, every person, every plant, animal, and tree had stopped, and was now focused on what was about to transpire. The world around us was not real anymore. Only this, this Crucifixion, was real.

Jesus appeared. As I looked at Jesus, I saw just how badly he had been beaten. Jesus had been disfigured and extremely weakened. His legs wobbled; he could not keep his posture straight. He was drenched in sweat. His left eye had been swollen shut. His jaw appeared to be disfigured. Gaping wounds covered his entire torso front and back. The rule was never to give a prisoner more than forty lashes because that is all one person could take. Now add, that he had to carry that cross, that heavy cross, for the rest of the way!

A Roman soldier on horseback barreled up the street pulling behind him, on a rope, a dirty wooden cross. We watched as the cross was dropped only a few yards from where Jesus was now standing. Others looked back over to Jesus; I stayed focused on the cross. I watched in slow motion as 200 pounds of wooden cross hit the dusty road. Tiny dirt tornados rose from the ground on impact. The cross appeared to come alive. I noticed that some of the wood had been planed while other parts still had bark on it. The grain on the wood took on a life of its own becoming darker and richer as it lay there in the street of death. At the ends of the cross, sap formed and slowly slithered towards the ground. It was like someone trying to hold back tears but failed and the floodgates opened. This tree, this cross, was alive.

How could this man possibly carry that cross, that massive cross in the condition he was in? The sweat, the blood, the disfiguration, was more than even I could bear. Anger intensified within me, within all of us.

Four guards lifted the cross and set it on Jesus' shoulder. One of the guards slapped Jesus on the back as he was walking away.

The final walk had begun.

As I was following along the route, trying to stay as close as possible to Jesus, I kept hearing, "Don't do it."

I heard voices directed at me coming from the crowd but when I turned no one was there.

Small children turned and looked at me and said, "Don't do it mister."

I rubbed my eyes, shook my head, and looked at the children again but they had turned away as if nothing had happened.

"Don't do it."

Am I imagining things? Voices from all around were telling

me, 'Do not interfere.'

I had Jesus in my sight while He started up the road. Paul and Sy were on the other side of the street, a bit closer to Jesus than I was. The Roman soldiers had orders to get Jesus to Golgotha and crucify Him until He died. In the state Jesus was in now, He would likely die on the way to the Crucifixion. The soldiers needed to carry out their orders and get Jesus to the Crucifixion, alive.

As Jesus struggled with the cross, I saw Him stumble and then fall. Some in the crowd got louder, taunting Him to get up, much like we would do with a prizefighter who had just been knocked to the mat. Others grimaced at the sight of Jesus because of the condition He was in. How could this man stand up let alone walk and carry that cross? Only a week earlier, on Palm Sunday, they had cried "Hosanna, Blessed is He who comes in the name of the Lord;" Now, they detested Him.

Jesus was on all fours trying to raise his leg to go forward as the guards interjected and belittled him while the crowd continued to torment Him. A woman emerged from the crowd with a cloth and water. While tears fell from her face, she bent down and wiped the face of Jesus.

"That's Veronica!" I said to myself. I moved quickly closer and saw the guards were also moving in to remove her from the presence of Jesus. Veronica's two sons also saw their mother and the guards and started to run toward her. It appeared that the boys were afraid that the guards might hurt their mother and they were running to save her.

As I quickly maneuvered closer, I saw this large figure emerge from the side and grab the hands of the two boys.

"It's Sy!" speaking under my breath.

Sy grabbed the boys and started to escort them back into the crowd to get them off the pathway and out of danger. Paul was also nearby.

At that moment, two guards on foot and one on horse grabbed Sy by the shoulders, stopping him. Sy had been in this situation before. While on tour in Iraq, the three of us had papers to locate an Iraqi national and return him to headquarters. We got word of his exact location but when we arrived, we were ambushed. They grabbed Sy for ransom, not knowing we were only a few yards away. We followed. They took Sy to their headquarters and before they could do anything to him, Paul and I wiped out the entire network. Yes, we are prepared if they take Sy away. He is not alone.

I could see Paul starting to feel for his weapons; just a double check that they were there and ready to be used.

"Let your boys be," shouted one guard to Sy.

"What's your name?" the other demanded.

Sy, pausing for more time, searched to make eye contact with Veronica. Sy saw her, and motioned for the boys to go to their mother.

"What's your name I say!"

"Simon, Sy... Sy..., Rene," stuttered Sy visibly shaken and trying to avoid any other contact with the guard.

The guard on horseback announced, "SIMON OF SYRENE WILL NOW BEAR THE CROSS!"

Sy was now turning and visually searching the crowd trying to locate either Paul or me for some type of guidance. Fear has never shown through the eyes of Sy before today but I could see now the terror in his eyes. He was perspiring profusely. For the moment, he is safe out in the public. He is a professional and he will adjust to these new circumstances.

"What the hell just happened?" I muttered to myself.

Do we need to put this plan in motion now? We would all surely be crucified. My mind was racing but again, where was it going? All the training could not have prepared us for this moment, these moments that were about to transpire.

Forced by the guards, Sy was led to the cross. His eyes were wide when he made eye contact with Jesus.

Jesus was kneeling on the ground next to the cross. Sy extended his trembling hand down to help Jesus up but the guards pushed him towards the cross and away from Jesus. Sy cautiously felt his weaponry and hoped that the guards did not suspect or feel anything that was under his tunic when they pushed him.

Sy, who now was in the presence of Jesus Christ our Savior, reached down on the ground to raise the blood-soaked, sweat-covered cross. The cross was a bit awkward for him to lift, as he fumbled with it.

Paul who was also close by in the crowd, emerged from the side to help raise the cross onto Sy's soldiers. As Paul began to help lift the cross, a guard with a ferocious whip, tagged Paul in the left forearm ripping tissue from his arm.

"Leave!" shouted the guard.

Paul let out a grueling noise and quickly fell to one knee. The guard again aimed his whip again at Paul and again ordered him to leave.

This time Paul caught the whip and tore it from the guard's hand. I had just neared the guard as this was happening and took that guard down by snapping his neck. I dragged him over to a nearby wall and placed him there as if he were sleeping. They were so focused on Jesus that no one in the crowd saw what transpired with the guard I had taken out. Paul got back on his feet and helped Sy maneuver the cross onto his shoulder.

It was a solemn moment when Sy, standing there holding Jesus' cross, extended his arm and reached out to Jesus, and Jesus looking at Sy, reached to take Sy's hand to get back on His feet. Jesus was unsteady. Sy stood firmly there, until Jesus collected His composure and was able to continue. At this point, Jesus was totally depleted. How He managed to make the distance is baffling to me.

After lifting the cross for Sy, Paul worked his way back into the crowd and again blended in and followed. Under his garb, Paul applied a bandage wrap to tuck in the torn muscle and skin to stop the bleeding and mend his wound.

Sy had adjusted to the change of plans and proved himself not only worthy to our team but to God Himself.

As they walked down the street Jesus turned slightly to Sy who was next to Jesus and told Sy to walk behind Him. Sy later told us, that Jesus, at that point told him, "This is God's will. Do not interfere, carry my cross. You are not setting your mind on the things of God, but on the things of man." There was a pause, then Sy dropped back a few steps.

Jesus then spoke to Sy one last time, "Stay near me Simon."

Sy responded, "Always my Lord, always." Sy knew at that moment, when Jesus had talked to him, that this mission was a no-go!

"Who has more authority than Jesus?" Sy thought.

We watched from the crowd as Sy and Jesus walked towards the Crucifixion. Sy walked behind Jesus, carrying His cross. Sy observed this man, Our Savior, continue to walk in agony, towards His Crucifixion and death. Sy painfully watched the trail of blood on the street from behind Jesus, and followed His footprints, as they worked their way to the place of the skull. Sy told us later that he had never been so humbled. Sy told us that he will never forget the conversation he had with Jesus.

"I will never leave His side."

Paul and I walked along the street following Sy and Jesus. They were being pelted with all kinds of liquid, feces, old food, and rocks. Paul and I had always been professional in our missions, only concentrating on what we were there to do. However, this was personal and we weren't too polite to the evil people on the street antagonizing and throwing objects at Jesus and Sy. Some of them got knocked over, some got hurt. People were shouting and screaming. "Death to the Blasphemer!" "There is only one God!"

By this time most of the people had turned against Jesus. The followers and believers had peeled off not wanting to witness the demise of Jesus. However, some of the very loyal were there until the end.

Sy had been picked by the guards because his skin color was different from the average person in the crowd. Plus, he happened to be in the wrong place at the wrong time. The guards knew he was not from around there based on his appearance. It was much easier to humiliate an outsider than it would have been a local. Thus, the guards picked Sy. As it turned out, Sy was in the right place at the right time.

The wailing of women's voices continued even louder as we got closer to the hill. The crowd had considerably thinned. The winds were beginning to pick up. The clear skies were no more. Jesus stopped again, with Sy pausing with Him.

"Daughters of Jerusalem, do not weep for me, but weep for yourselves and your children. For the days are surely coming when they will say. 'Blessed are the barren and the wombs that never bore and the breasts that never nursed.' Then they will say to the mountains, 'Fall on us, and to the hills, 'Cover us.' For if they do this when the wood is green, what will happen when the wood is dry?"

We neared the destination. This was the place of the Skull, Golgotha; it was a large mound with indentations on the front of the rocks that gave it the appearance of a skull hence how its name was derived.

The guards told Sy where to drop the cross on the ground.

I was right behind Sy. My body began to freeze up. My mind was alive and well-focused but I could not move. I felt like I was swooning. Everything began to spin and swirl.

"Drop the Cross!" yelled the guards.

Sy disobeyed the orders and turned to his left, carrying the cross, away from Jesus.

"Drop the Cross! Stop!"

What was happening? The extraction was on! I didn't know this was going to happen. Why did my guys leave me in the dark?

"I'm stuck. I can't move."

I watched as Sy, carrying the cross, began to walk increasingly faster and then started to run. Now, all the guards realized Sy was running away with the cross and they all started toward Sy. A guard on horseback raced to cut off Sy and stopped him while the rest of the guards were still running towards him.

Paul at this point with all the guards pursuing Sy, was alone with Jesus quickly preparing to move Him to safety.

With anger veins streaking across his face, Sy grabbed the base of the cross and began to swing the cross around and around. The momentum was increasingly faster with each spin. Sy then let out a battle cry as he released the cross striking the side of the horse and bringing the horse and the guard to the ground. The horse was severely injured, with a gaping hole just below the withers, struggled to get back on its feet, and then hurriedly limped off down the hill without its rider.

The guard, also injured, was confused and surprised by what was transpiring, that he was slow to react but finally reached for his sword. The guard had a bewildered look on his face as Sy reached for his gun, pulled out his 9 mm, and fired two quick bursts into the soldier. The guard fell to the ground as the other guards approached. Sy's tunic is now down to his waist exposing vividly every single muscle in his arms and upper body. One by one, two by two, the guards fell. The ones that didn't fall, ran. Paul, in tune with Sy, did the same. They each took out a smoke grenade and launched it toward the fleeing soldiers and parting nonbelievers.

The guards that fled, fled because they have never observed this much show of force and with weapons they had never seen. Paul quickly loaded up Jesus onto the stretcher and began to take Him towards the cart. Now, in slow motion, Paul and Sy carried Jesus on the stretcher towards His rescue. I am still frozen, unable to move. As Jesus passed me, I looked down at Him on the stretcher. Jesus' eyes opened up, "Noooooooooo!"

At that very moment, a guard thrust his spear into my back, and said, "Get out of the way."

I fell to the ground grimacing in pain. Paul made his way to me and asked "What happened?"

"I don't know. I guess I was just in a fog and stopped. I had a strange vision that . . . ."

"Come on over here and let me take a look."

"Looks like you might have cracked a rib or two. If it wasn't for the Kevlar, it would have been much worse."

"The Crucifixion, is it still on?"

"Sorry to say, yes."

"Where's Sy?" I asked as Paul looked at me kind of strangely.

"He's over there with Jesus, are you okay?"

"Yeah, not sure what just happened. Help me up."

I could barely stand; the pain in my back was intense.

"Let's get you out of here, there is blood coming out of your mouth."

"No, I am staying until the end."

I took a deep breath then we made our way closer to the site of the Crucifixion.

Sy had laid down the cross where the guard had told him. Sy looked at Jesus one more time. In an unfamiliar gesture in that era, Sy made the sign of the cross to Jesus. Sy then turned to walk away and wept. No words were spoken towards the end of their encounter, but through their eyes, Jesus was telling Sy, "I need to go through with this."

Through Sy's eyes, the reply was, "I know."

The skies became darker and the guards kept looking up to the sky as if they were expecting something supernatural to happen. The winds were now howling.

Sy walked away from the cross and toward us. With Sy's hand quickly passing his throat, he motioned to us that the mission was aborted. We waited for Sy to join us. Surprisingly out of the hundreds of people who had attended today, the trial and procession, there were just a few that remained. There were probably fewer guards here now, than had been around earlier.

"We cannot do this! I won't do this! This IS the will of God and we can't interfere." We must abort this mission, now! Let's go home."

Sy had never been this insistent about anything since we had all been together.

"We have never given up on a mission or failed a mission but I think Sy is right, let's go home," Paul chimed in.

"I agree. It's a done deal."

I turned and didn't say anything. My composure and my body language told the story. We were not defeated. God's will had taken over. We watched as Jesus was nailed to the cross. The guards were looking for help to raise the cross but got no volunteers from the crowd.

We knelt behind a small group of people that had gathered close to the cross, and prayed. We cried with them and prayed some more.

The sun faded. The clouds began to swirl. Total darkness filled the sky.

"My God, My God, why have you forsaken me," shouted Jesus.

"I thirst," He proclaimed.

A guard brought up some sort of sponge that had been dipped in something that seemed offensive to Jesus. The guard laughed when Jesus refused the liquid as it got closer to his lips.

Boy, I want to take that SOB out, I thought to myself.

"It is finished, Father into your hands I commit my spirit," Jesus then said.

Most of us were on our knees. When it was finally over, some of the guards realized what had just happened and they too fell to their knees. The darkness was mind-boggling; the winds atrocious. There was thunder and lightning like we had never experienced before.

We wept! It is over!

The people in the group that were closer to Jesus, embraced each other for comfort. The crying was heart-wrenching. We, the three of us, had just witnessed the death of our Lord and Savior Jesus Christ.

One of the guards approached Jesus on the cross and thrust a spear into his side. Liquid poured out onto the ground. There was no more movement on the cross. Some of the other guards approached and lifted the cross up in the air to take it from the ground then they gently laid it down. They treated Jesus so much more reverently after his death than before he was crucified.

The three of us sat in amazement at what we had just witnessed.

The guards backed away after setting the cross and Jesus on the ground. They let those close to Jesus have some privacy. From our studies, we assumed it was Jesus' Mother Mary, and Mary Magdalene at the cross when Jesus was taken down. Now, there were no evil or vile words spoken.

Some of the observers who were further back from the cross started to leave. There were a few others there that moved closer once Jesus was taken down from the cross. Some of them were beginning to wipe off the blood on Jesus' body to prepare it for burial. Mother Mary, took Jesus in her arms and held him and cried. We turned away out of respect for the family that was there and stepped back to a location that was not as close to the cross but still close enough to monitor the activities.

We felt so defeated, yet victorious. We did not complete the assignment that we were so willing to do. We watched as we saw Jesus being tortured and die on the cross. We witnessed the birth of Christianity!

When we return home, we would need to answer to the control center, but that didn't matter. We needed to answer to ourselves, we needed to answer to God. If there are other options, I think that we can return somewhere else in time and complete a mission similar. Then again, maybe we do not want to get involved in changing this at all.

Chapter 18

Lepros

As it approached 3 pm, all eyes were fixed on the monitors that read JOHN 19:30.

Lepros was soaked in sweat, unable to stay still. Lepros had his doctor at the facility to monitor his health conditions as they had drastically been deteriorating over the last few days. His doctor insisted he be on an IV.

"I don't have time for that nonsense," he barked.

By John 19:30 being removed from the Bible, it would be the only indication that the mission was a success.

At exactly 3 pm, the monitor went blank with current date and time still registering. In a state of shock and exaltation, Lepros looked around and saw Sid.

"We did it!" as he grabs his chest.

"Son of a Bitch, we did it!"

"Sid, tell me it's gone!"

"It's gone, Boss. The mission was a success. The camera is still live. You can tell because the time and date are still registering. See here, the seconds are still moving," said Sid pointing to the bottom of the monitor.

Lepros jumped up again, this time grabbing his doctor.

"Get the hell out of here," he said laughing incessantly. "I don't need you anymore."

Lepros went in front of his office camera and zoomed live to the entire building. He was on every screen available. "I have an announcement," uncontrollably gloating. "This mission has been a huge success and I want to thank each and every one of you. There is cake in the cafeteria. Let's shut everything down and we will see you all on Monday."

Lepros quickly switched back to the live feed from the Bible Museum in Washington D.C.

"Amazing, Sid, we did it. It's gone."

"Yeah Boss, the mission was a success."

"Any chance that there is a malfunction on their end?"

"No sir. It's a live feed. Date and time are still operable. There was no crucifixion."

The celebration started and every minute Lepros stared at the monitor, laughing out loud each time. The champagne flowed.

"Here's to Jesus!" Lepros shouted gleefully.

Some of the office personnel met in the cafeteria for the big celebration. The scientists and everyone who had some part in the project was there.

Everyone except Jimmy.

"Get that no-good bastard on the phone Sid, and tell him to be here Monday. He should have been here today!"

"I give him a lot of shit but it seems to bring out the best in him," he said laughing uncontrollably.

"Great job Sid!" as Lepros glanced at the monitor one more time.

"Let's go ahead and get our backers here on Monday."

"Sounds good Boss. I will get confirmations today."

Lepros could not stop laughing.

It was 6 o'clock Friday at the Bible Museum in Washington D.C. The cleaning crew was not aware that they had knocked over the camera that had a live feed over the Bible that was focused on JOHN 19:30. It wouldn't be discovered until Monday.

Chapter 19

Burial and Resurrection

The ninth hour had just passed. Jesus had been crucified and died. It will take some time but eventually, we'll learn to embrace 'the beauty of the cross.'

We had not been recalled so we each activated our rings.

"There must be some type of problem, don't you think, Cap? and...and, we need you to be looked at."

"I am ok Paul. I am worried about Sy. I have never seen him so down."

"This has been hard on all of us," Paul chimed back.

We watched as the body of Jesus was taken away. A couple of men that had appeared were directing the ones carrying his body. One of the men was probably Joseph of Arimathea, the one who had been allowed to take the body of Jesus and have a proper burial in a new tomb. They were not taking Jesus to the common grave of the criminals.

The location of the entombment was in a garden setting. The Garden Tomb, as it's referred to, is located in a small valley that covered maybe a couple of acres.

There was a ridge on this property all around the vale.

We had found an isolated spot on the ridge directly across from the tomb opening. Along this secluded area, there was a mix of bushes and trees, the perfect place for us to wait until we were recalled.

As we looked down from our location, we could see olive trees all around the grounds and flowers of every kind and the smell was refreshing and rejuvenating. There was an olive press near a small watering hole on the property. On the side of the garden was a mound, a stone mound. There was a cave-like opening in the stone side of the wall. This cave would be Jesus' tomb, for only a short while.

"This is really tranquil, peaceful," said Paul as we watched from our perch that surrounded the valley.

"Smell those olive trees, wow."

"Hey, Sy, this is some place don't you think?" I said, attempting to distract Sy from his thoughts he was having with the crucifixion.

"Yea," Sy replied softly, not really paying attention to the moment as he started to pace.

"Those other people down there, the ones with the baskets, they must be workers," said Paul.

"They're watching the same thing we are watching. Do you think they know who is being entombed?"

We watched as several people entered the cave, two that carried Jesus' body and three others who had entered with them.

"There's Mary and Mary Magdalene," uttered Paul.

It seemed like about half an hour when they emerged from the cave. Several Roman guards were on hand to maneuver the huge rock in front of the opening, sealing it from outsiders. Two white horses were being used to help pull the large hunk of granite to seal the opening.

As the horses began to work, the guards whipped them to pull harder, you could distinctively hear their hooves pound the earth repeatedly, trying to gain leverage, while the rock slowly worked its way closer to the opening. You could feel the ground tremble as the boulder moved ever so slowly leaving an indentation in the ground from where its journey had originated. The piece of the mountain moved only about 15 feet to its final destination but the guards and the horses appeared exhausted. The horses feasted on water while the guards had collapsed to the ground.

Flowers and lit torches were left outside, as people slowly dispersed. Night had begun to fall.

We had everything with us that we needed to make our return. Our equipment, clothing, almost everything we came here with, we are leaving with. As we anticipated our return to the modern day, we spread out just a bit but not too far from each other.

I noticed that Sy had ventured out from us further than I felt comfortable with, but reasoned with myself that he wanted some distance to digest all that had happened today. We were still within our designated time frame and our Control Center would most likely return us at any moment.

I was in pain and lying in the grass. I motioned for Sy to come here.

Sy, who by now was physically and mentally exhausted, walked over to us.

Before I could speak, Sy said, “I am not ready to go back just yet Mark. I’d like permission to go see Veronica.”

Sy was determined to see her again one last time.

“Of course, Sy. The only problem I see is if they call us back, you may just disappear as Veronica is holding you.”

“I’ll take my chances, sir.”

“Sy come on, chill, go see Veronica, we’ll be here.”

Paul and I, both in need of medical assistance, sat on the

beautiful ridge, reflected on our mission, and prayed.

"We have another mission now, Mark."

I looked at Paul.

"This new mission is from our Creator, God Himself. We need to share this event with the world."

"Ok," I chuckled, "but we are not supposed to remember anything."

"I don't want to forget any detail of this mission," Paul said insistently moving his head from side to side.

"I don't think we are going to have a choice there."

The time had passed that we were supposed to be returned; we were still in Jerusalem. If there ever were perfect weather, this would be it. There was so much tension in Jerusalem the last few days, but now there is calm.

Mission Control Center was probably processing our acknowledgment before they returned us home. Maybe there is a delay in that window of opportunity. I was searching for explanations on why we were still here.

Even though none of this was planned, we were not alarmed.

"What do you think they are doing back there?" Paul said referring to the Office.

"I know, hell if I know!"

"I am just saying, do you think they didn't bring us back because we didn't fulfill our end of the deal?"

"That's absurd Paul," I said even though I had been thinking the same thing.

Night came then the dawn. Sy had not returned from Veronica's. Paul and I had something to eat and awaited his return. Luckily, we each had an MRE in our tunic that we thoroughly enjoyed.

Paul was getting a little antsy now and said, "I am going to get Sy. This is ridiculous. He shouldn't be gone this long. What if something happened to him?"

"I agree. But I can't go with you," as I grimaced in pain.

About the time Paul was ready to leave, Sy walked up the ridge.

"Sorry guys for the way I acted before I left. Let's go home."

We each checked our rings at the same time. The small led was flashing on all our rings.

"They can retrieve us from anywhere, so let's just stay on the ridge here and wait," Paul said.

"I wouldn't want to be anywhere else."

Paul seemed to calm down knowing we all were together. We agreed to stay right where we were and we made ourselves comfortable.

"Guys, Veronica wanted me to give you this."

Sy reached into his tunic and brought out a large loaf of bread.

"She made this fresh and was hoping we all would have gotten together."

"My, oh, my!" Paul said as he reached for the loaf.

The tomb was located not too far from where the Crucifixion took place and close to where we had been staying. It was just a short jaunt for Sy to go see Veronica.

There was an occasional visitor to the tomb, that the guards would let in, but they never stayed long; whoever came, knelt, prayed, then left. The tomb was still well-guarded. Our position was perfect and surprisingly, no other people were around. We were far enough away from the tomb yet close enough to it to see what activity was going on around it.

There now were four guards, two on each side of the boulder in front of the tomb. I think with the beefed-up security, the

Jews wanted to make sure that no one would take the body of Jesus and claim his resurrection. Even though the tomb was protected by this massive boulder, I expected it would be guarded heavily until after the third day. The guards were very relaxed and did not appear to be standing at attention.

We had with us some water and rations as we waited to be taken back home. We watched the tomb intently from our position. There was no other activity around the tomb other than the guards who were replaced in the morning.

When we activated the rings to bring us home, a small beam of light emanated from the ring and started flashing. It continued flashing. We checked and double-checked and all three of our rings still appeared to be working. "What do you think?" questioned Paul.

"I don't know if I have those answers, Paul."

Sy again, started to get fidgety and restless sitting there with us.

"I keep playing back in my mind the words Jesus spoke to me. I don't know if he was mad at me when he said 'walk behind me' but I hope he knew I didn't want to harm him in any way. It's a lot that God has brought before me and I don't know how to digest it all. My heart is full."

"Believe me, God knew your intentions," I said.

Sy finally said that he wanted to see Veronica again because he never actually told her he was leaving.

"What do you mean you didn't tell her!" Paul barked.

I jumped in, "That's okay, go...go see Veronica."

I again reminded him that he could be called back at any moment, even a moment that they were together and that he would be gone. Sy said he would take that chance and just wanted to say goodbye.

"OK, buddy. Give her our regards. And thanks for the bread."

"He shouldn't be going now, but then again, I am not in charge," said Paul.

"What the hell does that mean? What difference does it make if he is there with Veronica or here with us?"

"I just feel better if he were here." Paul was sweating profusely. I removed his bandage and applied military-grade antibiotic ointment.

His forearm was severely infected and he was irritated. I assumed by the infection that some type of poison had been applied to the tip of the scourging whip.

The wound that Paul received from the guard was nasty. We treated the wound with the medicine we had brought for Jesus and rewrapped it. Paul said that even though the injury was quite severe, there was very little pain. He was weak. We buried the old bandages and other instruments we no longer needed. All these items were way ahead of their time for anyone to comprehend.

Anytime I moved, sat, stood, breathed, or spoke, I could feel a sharp pain in my back. There has never been a time in my life that I suffered this much.

"Cap, take these, it will help with the pain."

While we observed, some of Jesus' other followers tried to get onto the property but these guards chased them away. Some of the people who tried to enter looked familiar; I guessed that they were some if not all of Jesus' apostles. There were no other people near the ridge where we were camped out. This ridge would be a perfect spot for them or any of His followers, to come and observe.

Sy met with Veronica and they talked some more.

"Sy, what's wrong?"

"I am just trying to digest all that has happened today." Veronica puts her arms around Sy for the first time.

"I understand."

Sy eased away from Veronica and said, "Did you feel the same thing I felt when you were next to Jesus?"

"Sy, I felt so helpless. On the other hand, I felt very protected being in His presence. Even though He has died, I still feel that protection."

"Do you believe He is the Son of God?"

"I absolutely do!"

"The boys seem to have reverted back to when their father had died. This was very traumatizing for them today."

"Let me talk to them, I am sure I can bring them peace."

"You are a wonderful man, Sy. I know you may be leaving soon but I wish you could stay with us."

Sy felt ashamed and couldn't bring himself to tell Veronica the truth. He told the boys that they should always remember what happened to Jesus and the love their mother had shown Him, regardless of how she was pushed away by the guards. Sy suggested that someday soon they too pick up the cross that Jesus bore and help Him carry it through their lives. Sy explained that they may not understand right now but that the message Jesus has brought into this world would eventually come to them.

"Boys, Jesus has a cross-shaped plan for us, and one day you will embrace it."

He reiterated, "Never forget what happened on the street. You saw all the pain and the sorrow; but did you also see the love that was poured out? Jesus gave his life because he loved us!"

"Boys, Jesus will live again," Sy stated like a prophet.

When Sy spoke to her boys, a warm sense of affection enveloped Veronica. Sy had always given them the right advice and said the right things to them, and that was comforting to Veronica.

Much later, Sy wished Veronica a good day. "I need to go back to my friends; they will be leaving soon."

With tears beginning to flow and looking straight into his eyes, Veronica said, "Do what needs to be done."

She handed Sy some fruit and more bread as he headed back to the Garden Tomb.

Sy never told Veronica he was leaving.

Sy returned to the ridge. Paul and I were relieved to see Sy but greeted him with silence. We were not standoffish; we just didn't say a word. All three of us were totally exhausted, mentally and physically. Paul and I both needed medical attention. It was getting late and we had not yet been transported. We wanted to be here, to see where Jesus was buried and watch the activity around the tomb; maybe instinctively we knew it would be sometime before we were going home. If we weren't going home soon, we wanted to be front and center to witness the most important day in Christianity, The Resurrection!

Night passed on the second day. We were eagerly waiting because now, this was the beginning of 'The Third Day.'

Matthew 12:39-40; Jesus rebuked them saying: An evil and adulterous generation seeks after a sign of the prophet Jonah. For as Jonah was three days and three nights in the belly of the great fish, so will the Son of Man be three days and three nights in the heart of the earth.

With our training and all, staying awake at night was never

a problem for the three of us. We didn't dare start a fire at our location because the guards would have spotted us and taken us away and we were not about to leave, especially now. We each had taken intervals of stretching, walking, and watching. Our minds never stopped thinking of the ordeal that we put ourselves through. We also thought of the Glory we shared with Jesus the last couple of days. This is Christianity from the beginning!

The stars looked so clear tonight. Looking out we could see the hapless guards asleep next to the tomb. One guard looked like he was so distorted and uncomfortable that he almost looked like a cartoon character. Another lay flat on his back. The other two were not in sight. The three of us were used to night missions and were wide awake. This was the beginning of the Third Day. The anticipation was overwhelming.

In an unexpected moment, Sy said to Paul and me, "I love you guys." We both looked at Sy and nodded our heads, then dismissed his statement by looking back at the tomb.

The thought of going home now, was the furthest thing from our minds. Our thoughts focused on witnessing the Resurrection, firsthand! We concentrated on the tomb. Our hearts were beating at a record speed and we all gave the thumbs-up sign to each other.

"This is it guys!"

As we peered toward the cave, we saw a light start to glow from within. Peace and love began to flow through our bodies. It was a wonderful feeling. Paul stood up touching his body. "Are we going back? Is that what this feeling is?"

We could barely breathe. We were overwhelmed with excitement and anticipation. Time was standing still!

Matthew 28-2; There was a violent earthquake, for an

angel of the Lord came down from Heaven and, going to the tomb, rolled back the stone and sat on it. His appearance was like lightening, and his clothes were white as snow. The guards were so afraid of him that they shook and became like dead men.

The light illuminated all around the rock that had been placed in front of the tomb. The light got brighter and brighter. If you know the intensity of a bolt of lightning and how bright that is, you can magnify that tenfold and compare that to this light. The bolder of rock in front of the tomb started to crack. You could see the light pouring out from those cracks. The ground all around us began to rumble. The boulder moved from the front of the tomb over to the side, with some pieces of it crumbling to the ground; the guards looked like they were asleep!

We kept looking at the light until He appeared, Jesus, the King of Kings as He stood at the entrance of the tomb. So majestic! So bright and glowing! Jesus looked right at us. It was Him and us!

He nodded His head towards us in a positive way. Now, the light had become so extremely brilliant, we all, at the same time bowed our heads to shield our eyes because of the intensity. When I last looked down to my right where Sy had been next to me; I only saw his ring flashing as I closed my eyes. That was the last thing I remember.

Chapter 20

Preparation for the Big Announcement

"Everything has been arranged," Sid explained to Lepros in a very monotone voice. "We have 38 guests arriving in 32 aircraft. None of the guests will be coming by way of motorcade."

"Wonderful," replied Lepros. "I almost feel guilty," chuckling, "that the team couldn't be here with us to celebrate. Even if we had the capabilities to bring them back from the past..." now laughing.

"Sid, we just pulled off the greatest feat of all time and now, the world is ours. With this Jesus thing out of the way, I am in control of this planet," laughing whole heartedly.

"How should we present this to our donor partners?"

"Sid, this is a celebration! A full-blown party! From the time they set foot on our property till the time they leave! In our briefing... it will be just that, brief, and let's leave out the major details, about the team. We could say that the team met its demise after they completed the mission...and...they didn't return!"

Lepros went on, "Oh my, Sid, I haven't laughed this hard in years."

"You made them believe that by keeping Jesus from the cross they could save humanity, and save Christianity," Lepros mumbled and chuckled under his breath.

"Sid, I have to hand it to you, you are the greatest bullshit artist of all time," Lepros, now ungovernably laughing.

"He had been my biggest obstacle in this world. Him, and the church, and those believers! With no Crucifixion, there could be no Resurrection. With neither of those, there are no more believers! His legacy, even if he has one now, was just being another false prophet!" now acting quite pleased, and boastful with his accomplished feat.

"Look at the monitor; John 19:30, its gone. It's possible there is no more bible," Lepros laughed until it hurt.

"I will be their new god," jumping to his feet, standing and waving his arms high over his head like a kid at the carnival.

"They will come to me for food, water, and electricity; every basic need. I will control the masses! I will tell them where they can live and how they shall live. It's me or death for them. I've given money to many politicians to further my agenda, those useful idiots: now it's time to reap my rewards.

"One country at a time Sid! This was so much easier than trying to get God out of the classrooms and out of public places. It was easier than trying to take down churches and places of worship," Lepros now boasting.

Lepros, continuing to laugh, "Sid, how about when you gave them those rings...and told them they would be transported back when the rings were activated! Brilliant Sid, brilliant."

Sid squirmed in his chair, clumsily dumping the folders that were on his lap to the floor. Feeling irritated he jumped up. "I better get going to make sure everything is ready for the meeting."

Sid stooped to the ground and frantically tried get all his paper work that had fallen, together, for a quick and hasty exit.

"Sid, hold on! Sit down. Sit down I said."

Sid slithered back into the chair like a dog that had just been scolded, still tucking paper into the folders.

"Sid, you don't seem overly pleased..."

"Boss, I 've been with you a long time. This...this is getting to me now. We lied to those guys! I lied to them! I said I went back in time! I told them I saw Jesus and we would bring them back!" Sid now lurched back up on his feet, pointing at Lepros. "Why, because Jesus was too much competition for YOU! They never agreed... no one would have ever agreed to a one-way mission! Those guys are out there...waiting for us! Now!"

"You told them that because I pay you well! Besides, three useless lives for world power, Sid. Look at it as collateral damage."

Lepros' eyes were ablaze, his voice rose.

"We have funded riots and wars. We have funded protests and the fall of governments. We have changed currencies. We have corrupted criminal justice systems. We had turned people against each other. People have died because of it! You weren't too concerned when that happened!" Lepros stated angrily.

"I was face to face with those guys! They were decent people! I looked them in the eye and lied to them!"

"They're probably dead by now anyway Sid," Lepros scoffed and looked away. "It's time to move on, there's nothing we can do to change that now; even if we wanted to."

His demeanor softened.

"On a good note, Sid, maybe this will make you feel better," in a slithering, devious voice, rubbing his hands together as if it were a big payday, proclaimed, "Jesus is still alive!" as Lepros rocked ecstatically back and forth in his chair bellowing in gut wrenching laughter.

Now almost physically unable to speak, and all caught up in

himself, with the laughter sucking up all his energy, Lepros began waving both his hands and pointing towards the door, motioning for Sid to leave, then finally catching his breath he yelled.

"You have work to do. Go on, get out of here!"

Chapter 21

The Return

I raised my head to find myself lying in a bed, alone in a room that looked like it was a part of an old farmhouse. I just knew I was back. I felt like myself again. There was a lamp on the dresser with a cord leading to an electrical outlet. There was a light switch on the wall. I was surprised that the Control Center had returned us to this type of location, but I knew we were back, somewhere. I expected to return right to the Office where we had left. As I think back, oddly, our return location was never brought up during training.

I looked around momentarily to see where Paul and Sy were but didn't see either one of them. It was like I was waking from a terrible dream. 'Of course, the mission was real I said to myself. I remember it all...' I paused for a long time thinking about what I just said, 'I remember'.

I hastily rose from the bed to find that my garb and sandals had been removed and folded next to the bed on a chair.

I didn't have the severe pain in my back and turned to look into the mirror that was in front of me, still in disbelief that the wound was gone. I noticed that the area on my back was slightly discolored. A yellowish color much like the final healing of a bruise had covered the area where I had been hit by the spear of a Roman soldier. I thought that maybe I had been out for some time because of how severe my injury was and how far it had come along.

My ring, our return responder, was no longer on my finger either. There was a robe on the bed which I grabbed and put on. I took a deep exaggerated breath in hopes it would help me to calm down. Looking out the bedroom window I saw beautiful mountains and greenery and blue skies.

'Wow', I thought to myself standing there trying to figure out just where we were.

I knew now I was not in Nevada.

The smell of bacon, my favorite food, was in the air.

I walked out of the room and looked around. I was in some sort of older house. There was a long hallway with well-polished wooden floors. There was paneling up half the wall and patterned wall paper covering the rest. I noticed two country-style ceiling lights but neither was lit. My room was at the far end of the hallway, the furthest from the stair case. Looking down this hallway I could see doors, four of them, all closed, seemingly to other rooms. I could tell I was on the upper floor because of the stairway. At each end of the hallway were widows that beautifully framed out the countryside around us. I felt very much at home and at ease. It was peaceful and quiet.

The stairs were down at the other end, so I walked ever so cautiously, following the smell, towards the stairs, to begin my descent. I went down a couple of steps then stopped; then slowly, a couple more; and bending over, I could see part of the kitchen area. I heard humming coming from the kitchen. There was someone near the stove preparing the bacon I was smelling. As I got to the bottom step, a man turned around with a pan in his hand and a smile on his face and said, "Good Morning, Captain."

The man in the kitchen was Gabe himself. My first thought

was I was in awe that the mission Control Center never told us that Gabe was a part of this mission. Seconds after those thoughts crossed my mind, Paul emerged from the second floor, standing on the stairs, a couple of steps in back of me.

"Good morning, sir," Gabe uttered to Paul.

Paul seemingly a bit agitated said, "Gabe, what's going on and where are we?"

Paul and I waited a few seconds and waited for Sy to come down the stairs too.

Gabe felt that anticipation from us also and asked us to have a seat.

"Gabe, what are you doing here?"

"Where's Sy?" demanded Paul.

"You boys must be hungry," said Gabe trying to smooth over the contentment that was starting to fill the air.

"Why didn't you tell us that you were a part of our mission?"

"You are, right? We can't be back in Nevada?" I questioned.

"Where's Sy? Is he still upstairs?" as I started to turn to go upstairs.

"Boys! Please!" shouted Gabe, stopping me right in my tracks.

"I was not a part of your mission; you were a part of mine. I do not work for the company that sent you there."

I was now focused and listened intently to what Gabe was about to say. We were puzzled.

"Go on, who do you work for?" I said to Gabe.

"I work for the Man Himself, The Almighty, Our Father in Heaven. My job was that I had to go and convey a message to you boys, that Jesus needed to die on the cross for all the sins of humanity. But, for my mission to be successful, it had to be your choice whether to abort your 'mission' or not. You boys made a wise decision."

"Who are you?" I said.

"My name is Gabriel, Gabriel Malak. 'Malak' is Angel in Hebrew. To make it less complicated, I am the Angel Gabriel."

Paul's face was traumatized; frozen! He became white and I was wondering if he was going to pass out.

I was in total awe. "Tell us more! All of it! And where's Sy?" I said again.

"How long have we been here?"

"Just a short time, a couple of hours if you want to be exact," said Gabe.

"Gabe, we witnessed the Resurrection, closed our eyes then. . . here we are?"

"That sounds about right. Boys, please...Let's go outside and get some fresh air and enjoy some of this beautiful Vermont weather." Gabe proclaimed somberly.

Paul and I rushed out to the front porch, a painted wooden porch that wrapped around two sides of this well-maintained house. There was a beautifully crafted table with matching chairs, rockers and a swing. All very appealing.

"What do you want from us and where is Sy?" I boldly repeated.

"Sit down fellas, please."

We took a seat at the table since it felt a little more formal for discussion.

"Oh, where was I...," as Gabe stalled to collect his thoughts.

"Yes, yes, now Sy, falling in love with Veronica and protecting Rufus and Alexander from the guards, got caught up in the actual Crucifixion, documented in the Holy Bible. He became part of the story of Jesus."

"A certain man from Cyrene, Simon the father of Alaxander

and Rufus, was passing by on his way in from the country, and they forced him to carry the cross." Mark 15:21

"Since Sy was protecting Rufus and Alexander the guards assumed he was their father. The guards were not too bright, as you both well know. That's partly how they got Sy's name wrong also. When they asked him what his name was, he said, "Simon, Sy, Rene." The guards couldn't put that together so they announced 'Simon of Cyrene!'"

"Sy did a wonderful feat for Jesus and mankind. It was from his heart. Sy said he never wanted to leave the side of Jesus. He didn't."

"You are losing us Gabe. Please explain a little clearer."

"Before you three left Jerusalem that morning, Sy had weighed in what his life would be like back here without Veronica, vs. the life with Veronica and her two sons. Sy decided on the latter."

"I had a feeling he was getting too close to her," said Paul.

"It wasn't up to us." I fired back, a little irritated.

"It was also his chance to stay close to Jesus for at least a while and he did just that. After carrying the cross and being with Jesus there was no way he was going back. God was quite pleased with his choice to stay. When you two were returned, Sy, by choice, stayed. He went to Veronica and they gathered the two boys. They followed Jesus while he walked the earth for another forty days. Sy knew from reading the Bible where Jesus would appear and managed to be there with Him when He did. 'Stay close to me' Jesus said to Sy on the road to the Crucifixion. During the 40 days He told Sy to 'Feed my lambs.' Sy did both until the end." Paul continued.

"They followed Jesus to Bethany and after the Ascension, Sy and Veronica headed back to Africa and continued with God's work by 'Feeding His lambs.' After arriving in northern Africa, at Veronica's home, they started their ministry. They had a great life. Sy was a great husband and father as was Veronica a wife and mother. Sy turned out to be a wonderful step father to those two lads."

"Gabe, you said had and was!"

"We were together just hours ago. You are talking forty days after the Resurrection? I don't think we are comprehending. We were sent back just after the Resurrection."

Paul and I both edged up out of our chairs, in shock as Gabe continued. Paul began to pace shaking his head and acted like he didn't want to hear the rest of what Gabe had to say.

Gabriel chuckled, still seated, "You two know how much Sy liked his beef, so he started up a cattle farm in northern Africa, Libya we now call it. A small farm, big enough to feed his family and community. It was his hobby that he loved. Sy fed them, physically and spiritually."

"So. . . where is he. . ." Paul said to Gabe.

"Wait, wait, what do you mean started a farm in Africa?"

"I am totally confused," said Paul.

"Boys, that was two thousand years ago, this is now!"

Paul looked over at me in disbelief.

I put my hands on my head wondering if this was even real. Looking at Paul and his reaction to Gabe makes me assume he was feeling just as bewildered as I am.

"Sy continued to preach to the locals and converted many of them to Christianity. Veronica's two boys, after witnessing the death of Jesus, and having Sy and their mother as great inspirations and role models, went on to be disciples of Jesus and are attributed to many ministries in the region where they lived. You boys may not understand all this now but let me continue."

"Come on Gabe..."

"I stayed in close contact with Sy for the rest of his life. He lived many years, over a hundred, way beyond the expected life span as you now refer to. Sy talked to Veronica and myself about you two all the time. On his deathbed, those around him that never heard of you two, were puzzled when Sy started talking about special ops and jumping out of planes, My goodness!" Gabe chuckled.

"Those people thought he had lost it! They didn't know what a plane was. Sy is telling them how he jumped from the sky, quite amusing I must add. I know you both are still trying to figure this out, but there is so much more and this is where it may start to become a bit more complicated for you to understand."

"Is Sy dead?"

"Just give it to us. We'll have to digest it all anyway," said Paul

"Boys, I am an angel. Do you consider me dead?"

The day went on and we continued asking questions about Sy. We were slowly accepting the idea that Sy was no longer with us.

Paul and I sat outside while Gabe was inside the house.

"It feels like we are in mourning, like we are at a funeral," declared Paul.

"It feels pretty dark. Sy is not here; in so many words, we are told he is dead."

"I think it's just the two of us now Mark."

"Do you trust Gabe?" Paul asked.

"As bleak as things seem right now, yes! Paul, look at your scar. It was severely infected just hours ago. Its healed. My back, broken ribs, I have no pain. Yes, I believe Gabe...or should I say, Angel Gabriel."

"I mean no disrespect for Gabe. He is answering all our questions and in addition to, giving us more information than we asked. He seems to be openly honest!"

Afternoon passed into evening. Gabe had asked us to come inside and prepare for dinner.

"I have given you two a whole lot if information. But now, we need to discuss what your mission is from here on out. You need to be well fed and rested before we continue."

Paul and I went upstairs and changed into some clothes that had been placed in the dressers for us. 'Not a surprise I thought, that everything fit us perfectly.'

"This whole thing is just crazy," I shouted from my room across the hallway. "We should probably just take a step back and listen a little more, before we speak."

Paul peeked his head around the doorway in my room and added, "You're right. *Pause...* Ok, let's take a deep breath and see what Gabe's got to add."

I was slowly accepting reality; or is this reality?

We anxiously returned downstairs to continue this conversation with Gabe.

He was in the living room awaiting our reappearance. It was about four in the afternoon and it smelled like there was a turkey cooking in the kitchen.

"If that's turkey, I am all in," Paul said to me.

As soon as Paul and I set foot in the living room, Gabe picked up right where he left off.

"The inventor of the time device, that you boys used to get to Jerusalem, is Don McDaniel. Don is a genius and, in his youth, built many programs on computers; programs that reached out beyond the realms of reality. Space, galaxies, blackholes and things of that nature. He was intrigued with time and dimension. He determined through his scientific studies, that black holes warp the space and time around them. Together, it's called spacetime.

"He figured out that by using the black hole formulas and applying it to this world, he could generate time travel, here! On the other hand, he also found it challenging to hack into computers. Not just any computers, he started to hack into government computers, the ones that held highly top-secret records. Don soon got caught and charged. A plea deal was reached. He was a genius."

"Tell us more Gabe."

"In their in-depth investigation, the government was so intrigued by what Don knew and attempted to accomplish, that they ultimately hired him to work with a group of computer wizards on a top-secret Artificial Intelligence Project. The government invested more money in AI than it did on the space project. Only a few people in the government were privy to the AI division and hardly any of them knew what they were up to."

"Time travel!"

"Yes," echoed Gabe.

"The government had a top-secret project? Shocking!" said Paul sarcastically.

"Most didn't even know the project had existed, including the President of the United States."

"Sounds like a rogue operation, run by a shadow government that had an ulterior motive."

"Somehow, through underground sources, the word got out about the American Project and it drew much interest, amongst the dubious, much like Area 51 in Nevada. The people, the science geeks, that were hands on, 30 of them, who had been working on this time machine project, were starting to leave and took positions offered by the highest bidder for their talents.

"The government tried to stop them but because this project was so clandestine, they didn't have the resources to stop them from leaving. Top computer geeks working on the project were leaving left and right. The government's project, not completed, eventually fell to the wayside. Most that worked on the project only knew bits and pieces. Don knew the entire project inside and out."

"So, he would be the guy that I would want if I were building a time machine!" yelled Paul.

"Exactly," replied Gabe.

"The government device was not perfected but in some dark shrouded corners of the world, the thought of it, a time machine, drew attention from people with evil intentions and who had money. They were intrigued by the thought of time travel. They wanted the creators. Artificial Intelligence brought out the evil in the world. For most, this was the final piece for power; control over everything. Lots of it! After allegedly leaving the federal agency, and sworn to secrecy, Don was recruited by no other than Jake Lepros. He had money! He wanted Don and got him.

"While he was employed by the government, Don secretly built an experimental device in his garage, one that mirrored that same project he had been working on. No one knew he had it."

"How did he keep all that quiet?"

"Lepros offered Don a large amount of money to build the device, the time machine, and work for the Lepros foundation at the location you boys were at originally in Nevada. Lepros appointed Don as a Partner/Consultant to continue to experiment with the time device with unlimited resources.

"Lepros trusted no one including Don, so Lepros appointed an assistant for him, someone to watch over him and report back to Lepros. Don and the assistant, worked closely together, continuing to build and refine this time machine."

"That's amazing."

"From his early years, Don had envisioned the wonders of time travel. Now, with his mind, and the tools derived from Artificial Intelligence, he knew he could make this happen. And he did."

"We are living proof!" chimed Paul.

"As this project continued to grow and develop, Don learned that Lepros had intended to use it only for his personal gain. Don discovered that Lepros wanted to send some people back in time and take out key figures from our history, starting with Jesus. This is not what Don had intended his invention to be used for."

"So, Don was a good guy?"

"You got it!" said Gabe.

"After discovering what Lepros had planned to do with the device, Don began to take copies of his software and download them onto his home computer much like he did when he worked for the feds. Don wanted to contact authorities but, after working for the government, he didn't know what agency to trust. Don also understood that if he left Lepros, his life would be in danger."

Gabe sitting back and chuckling, "It turns out, the authorities already were aware of what was going on with the Lepros Corporation. They didn't know the extent of just what he was attempting to do but nonetheless, they were on to him. They knew that Lepros had the finances and would be seeking the power."

"Your friend Darby, your supersleuth tried to contact you fellas."

"How do you know about Darby?"

"His call to you had to be diverted, diverted by me."

"Why did you do that?"

"Various reasons Mark. If his message got into the wrong hands, surely the three of you would have been killed. Secondly, God wanted the three of you to attest to the Crucifixion of Jesus. God's mission."

"Why us Gabe?"

"I will get back to you on that one."

"Don was meticulously programming the Lepros computer to do, time travel and copying the same files onto his computer. Even though he was paid handsomely by Lepros, Don had minimal opportunity to beef up his equipment at home. He could not compete with the hardware and software Lepros had at his complex. When you three were hired by Lepros and had your bodies scanned, Don took a copy of that information for his private computer. Don knew way before that this was going to be a one-way mission for you three. Don wanted to be able to undo or counter anything the Lepros time machine did."

"How did he know that?"

"We weren't going to be brought back?" Paul exclaimed in a shocked voice.

"There was no program, at least on the Lepros computer, to retrieve anyone or anything back! The machine had not reached that level of perfection. Don had tested the equipment but sent back in time, only things, not people. He was not 100% certain that anything would go to a designated place in time. Don checked and rechecked his calculations. He was quite excellent in math and physics, and on paper, everything would seem to have worked."

"So, you're saying that this device was never proven?"

"Sorry to say, you're right," answered Gabe stoically.

"When you three were sent back, based on the input, you should have been in Jerusalem in the year of our Lord. But still, Don had his doubts with no way of verifying."

"We know that part worked!" said Paul.

"Don would like to know that someday," said Gabe.

"Jimmy, Sid, and Lepros, they all lied to us."

"Lepros wanted the job done now and didn't want to wait until the machine was capable of the return trip."

"Boys, even if he had those capabilities, he would not have returned you for the job he wanted you to do!"

"Why, are we..."

"Let me finish, Don wanted the chance to be able to bring you three back without Lepros knowing, using his computer in his garage. When you three were sent back in time, Lepros shut down the equipment in Nevada. Everyone in the Control Center was sent away except those playing around with the tracking devices. When Don returned to his house, he immediately prepared to bring you three back. He, had been working on the program to return anyone back from the past. It wasn't perfected but it was the best he could do for what he had at his disposal. Follow me boys on this," Gabriel added.

"Like I had said, Don's computer in his garage was not as sophisticated, or as powerful, as the one that Lepros had. Don programmed, or at least attempted to, his home device for a return from the past. In his endeavor, Don's computer scanned files and files of history on every parallel looking for the three of you. Don located Sy but not you two."

"How did that happen?"

"How did he find Sy and not us?"

"Don may have concluded that you two boys may have been killed or something like that. He was puzzled. What he didn't know was that he had some wrong information."

"Don proceeded to bring Sy back."

"And?"

"One major problem," Gabriel had a long pause, "Don was searching for you three on the wrong parallel! He was a hundred years off! That's why he could not locate you two! You two were already back here. But he found Sy. You two were no longer there, at least not on that parallel."

"Where is he? Where's Sy?"

"Sy lived for about a hundred years after Jesus' death. If you read books written about Sy, apocryphal books, they say he was martyred. They claim his body was sawed in half. That is how he died. At least that is how it was reported how he died. . ."

"Oh, my Lord."

"Boys, I was there with him. He was ready to die before this extraction even took place. Believe me, when he passed, he was not in any pain. In reality, Don's machine was not working as he thought it should work. Don had bad intel on his computer. He tried to extract Sy from the past back to the present. Since he was off by a hundred years, only parts of Sy's 100-year-old body matched the original scan which was 100 years earlier. Only a part of Sy's body came back. The other part of his body was left there hence, Simon was martyred 'his body was sawed in half.'"

Somberly, Gabe said, "Sy lived a great life. He fulfilled God's mission."

Tears started to fall from Paul's eyes.

I needed to turn away.

Chapter 22

Mission Second Half

"Your mission was very, very successful, in God's eyes, the first part of it anyway."

"What do you mean the first part?"

"You may have accepted a job for Lepros with pay, but unbeknownst to you, that was only God using those people to fulfill His mission."

"Tell us Gabe."

"The second half of His mission for both of you is to go out and share the word of God. Our preachers here now, in the present, preach from faith. You two will be preaching from first-hand knowledge. You both will preach about the final days as if you were there."

"We were...," said Paul.

"Exactly. Share with the world the pain that Christ felt, and describe each step he had taken in the end. You two are first-hand disciples, 2000 years after the Crucifixion. You two are the ONLY living witnesses to Jesus Christ, the Crucifixion, and the Resurrection."

"Tell the world about our time travel?"

"No. Tell them about the love of Jesus."

"Wait, we were told we would not remember anything when we returned. I remember everything!" Paul nodded in agreement.

"That was a bunch of bull crap," snickered Gabe.

"Me too, and look here is my wound from the Crucifixion," raising his left forearm up to show us. Look Mark! It's healed; it's only a scar."

"Boys, according to CP Industries, you were never supposed to be returned." Gabriel chuckled, "you were not brought back by your mission center. They were unwilling and incapable of doing that! God returned you! God returned you here! God's mission for you two is far from complete. But now you must finish the rest of your assignment that He and He alone has laid out for you!"

"Gabe what is it, what does He want us to do?"

"You have been with Jesus, seen Jesus, touched him, saw a miracle, seen him put to death, and watched Him Rise. You have knowledge to share boys. You two are the only live witnesses to Jesus. This is how you will save Christianity! This is how Christianity will be saved! God has allowed this for you both, to spread His Word here and now."

"But you will receive power when the Holy Spirit comes on you; and you will be my witnesses in Jerusalen, and in all of Judea and Samaria, and to the ends of the earth." Acts 1:8

Gabriel got up and headed towards the kitchen.

"It's almost dinner time."

Paul and I sat in bleakness, contemplating what we just heard.

When Gabriel returned, he brought with him a newspaper. He again sat down with us. As we both glanced at him, Gabriel opened the newspaper towards his face in a demonstrative way.

"Tragic isn't it, says here a helicopter and private jet collided at a remote office complex center about an hour north of Las Vegas, Nevada. Sources say several have died and it appears most of the complex was destroyed by numerous explosions.

Mm... It goes on to say that a number of the world's elite, may have been part of the casualties and may have been gathering for some type of conference. Pity! Ongoing investigation is under way. Amazing!" as Gabe continued to read.

"What? Let me see that!"

Gabe located the story and continued. "Local authorities, Nevada State Police, NTSB, FBI and branches of the military are on the scene. Mark, what's your take?"

"With all those agencies present, we are not getting accurate information."

"Lepros?" questioned Paul.

"This modern-day transportation is not what it should be. Give me a horse or a mule anytime," as Gabe tried diverting the suggestive question.

"Gabe, did you say numerous explosions? Does it say how many have died?"

"Nope, I guess, as they say, tune in tomorrow," said Gabriel trying to gloss over the inference.

"Can one air traffic disaster set off numerous explosions? Mark, we've been there, that place is spread out," said Paul.

"Jimmy!"

"What do you think?"

"He set us up."

"You know he was a bomb tech in the military."

"So, he said."

Chapter 23

Next

Paul and I were speechless! God had used this fraudulent company that had dragged us in to do their dirty work so that we three would be able to do His work. *Brilliant,* I thought. *It's a miracle.*

Things were beginning to sink in.

Paul and I sat there still numb but things were slowly starting to be absorbed and digested by us. The thought of us without Sy was depressing.

"God wants us to do what no one else has done for over 2,000 years. He wants us to spread the word from first-hand knowledge. He wants us to tell the story like we were there," uttered Paul.

"We were there!"

"It still seems so unreal," said Paul. "Maybe I will wake up soon then be able to laugh about it."

"It's real. This is all real."

"According to Gabe, Sy had already completed his end of the deal with God. I still can't believe that Sy was right next to me just hours ago and now he's gone."

"Gabe, what does God want us to do now?"

"Preach!"

"I have never spoken in front of a group before."

"Oh, my dear Paul. You won't be speaking in front of a

group, you will be speaking to masses, hundreds, thousands of people. God wants you to have a large audience."

"But I never. . ."

"Don't worry, you will be ready."

Mark 16:15; "Go into all the world and preach the gospel to all creation."

Still somewhat shocked by the events over the last couple of weeks, I leaned over to Paul placing my hand on his shoulder, "Paul, when we go out and share the story of Jesus, we must always, always include Sy in every thought we put forward."

Paul replied, "Don't worry, that's a given."

"Sy will be with us every step of the way."

Gabe went upstairs and soon returned.

"This is for the both of you," Gabe said as I unfolded a cloth.

"What's this?"

"Veronica had given that to Sy. When Sy was dying he asked me to give it to you guys."

I opened it up all the way.

"He said when the time was right, you two would know what to do with it."

Paul drew closer and looked at the material. It was the veil Veronica used to wipe the face of Jesus.

The entire image of Jesus' face, in detail was on that cloth.

"I had heard about the shroud of Turin. That bears the complete image of Christ, his burial shroud."

"Mark, I had read sometime back that there are two clothes in different locations, both claiming to be the real Veil of Veronica."

"Where are they?" said Paul.

"One article said the veil with the image was stored in the chapel in the southwest pier supporting the dome at St. Peters

Basilica in Rome."

"What about the other?"

"The other veil was supposedly secreted, hidden and taken away from Rome after it was sacked and plundered in the 1500 hundreds, by orders of Pope Clement VII. Supposedly it's now in Abruzzo, Italy and has been for the last 500 years."

"What did Sy mean, Gabe, when the time was right?"

"You boys will have to figure that one out but not now, we have way too much work to do."

Paul and I looked at each other, not knowing what to say.

"We have the real Veil. Is it up to us to share it with the world? The image of Christ was put on this cloth just days ago."

"No one would understand," I said to Paul.

"When the time is right, just like Sy said."

Chapter 24

Second Half of the Mission. Continued.

Gabriel continued on like a drill instructor and said, "I arranged a meeting with several religious leaders in the area. That's the place where we will begin."

"Don't worry," he said, "the audiences will keep getting larger and larger. They will come to hear you."

We arrived in downtown Burlington. Paul nor I had anything prepared. We met leaders from both the Roman Catholic Diocese of Burlington, Beth EL Synagogue, the Episcopal Diocese of Vermont, the Zen Center, members of Union Baptists Church and leaders from Kingdom Hall. Forty people all together agreeing to listen to what we had to say. Other denominations were represented also. Gabe joined us and was in his usual jovial mood.

Little did the leaders know that we had just been in the presence of our Lord Jesus Christ, and had just witnessed the Crucifixion and Resurrection.

"We want to share a message with as many people as possible."

"Even though we have not been ordained, by the Grace of God and the Holy Spirit we need to share our message. His message," Paul said.

"How did you get this so-called message?" asked one of the leaders.

Gabe stood up and smiled at the group, cleared his throat and said, "From a very reliable source."

That's all they needed to hear. Gabe had a way of swaying people. We continued to speak to the group from our hearts. We had a lot of help from above because the leaders were surprisingly receptive.

While Paul was speaking, one of the leaders he had been sitting next to, looked down at his arm and noticed his scar.

Gasping for air he said, "Mr. Jenkins, I apologize but I noticed your scar. How in Heavens name did you get that?"

With a genuine beaming smile, he replied, "I was just helping a friend."

For these meetings and future events, we never took any prepared lectures with us, ever. Preaching was not on our things-to-do list prior to all this, but now, it sure seemed so natural when we did. The leaders liked what they heard from us and each of them booked us into different churches and venues in the area.

Chapter 25

The Assignments

Most of the time Paul and I went our separate ways to spread the Word. When we would enter an establishment to talk, the Grace of God and the Holy Spirit fell upon us. Our sermon had always started quite calmly. However, when we were finished we were drained. We both gave it our all and it all came out! At the end of each sermon, we were physically and emotionally exhausted. We easily recovered to go on to the next venue.

"Hey Mark. Do you think we will ever get invited to Lakewood in Texas?"

"If God wants us there, we'll be there."

We first got a lot of local attention. After hearing our sermons, some people started putting things on the internet and how our message changed their lives. The momentum began to build. People were again interested to hear the Word and the message we were delivering.

From local to state, then national, then international; we were in demand. We started in Vermont then New Hampshire. By the time we preached in Maine, we were soon invited to Quebec, then Ontario. We had spread out and were hitting most of the lower forty-eight. Paul and I were old school. We initially had no websites, blogs or podcasts. Soon we had 'groupies for Jesus.' They came complete with t-shirts and merchandise. All profits were donated to local charities.

We attended each event, in person, never missing an engagement. This past winter a record snowstorm hit the Twin Cities area. We were both scheduled to speak, right in the heart of that storm. In almost white-out conditions, we left the airport and started to follow a plow on the highway. For some unknown reason, the truck led us the entire way, twenty-nine miles, directly to the Cathedral of St. Paul, then continued without stopping. When we arrived, it appeared on the outside that everyone decided to stay home. We were surprised when we entered, that the Cathedral was packed and they rose to give us a standing ovation.

About a week after this engagement, we were told that our prayers had helped cure a woman of stage four cancer, who had driven there with her family from Michigan. Many people over the next several months have written that miracles, like the one mentioned, had been happening to them also. God had truly blessed us, and given us a gift to share.

We both went about from place to place and Gabe was right, we were soon booked all the time. Gabe was always around when we needed him. If we had a question or wondered about anything, Gabe would show up and have a lengthy discussion with us. He had all the answers we needed. He was our new best friend.

We were invited to the Cathedral of St John the Divine Episcopal, located in Manhattan, New York City. My Brothers and Sisters in Blue were in full force, directing traffic and monitoring the large crowd for their safety and ours. It was not unusual to receive threats from reprobates. Today was no exception.

It was a majestic church built with stone, granite, and

limestone on the outside and even more impressive on the inside with the famous rose window immediately catching your eye upon entry. The Cathedral boasted 121,000 square feet of floor space, the world's sixth-largest church. The attendance for this evening's presentation was estimated to be about 8,000 people, inside. There are television screens on the outside for those who cannot make it inside. Paul and I were both together, at this event. We each had a podium, on either side of the altar. People had traveled from all over the world to hear what we had to say. Over just a few short months we had attracted the attention of many believers and some curious non-believers. Not everyone there wanted to share the glory. There were occasionally, people from the other side, skeptics and anti-Christians. We had also attracted the attention of the Deep State.

"Greetings From Our Lord and Savior Jesus Christ. Through us, He sends to all, His love."

The church reverberated with a polite scattered applause.

"I saw this picture the other day on the internet. It had on it a crucifix with the words, 'I asked Jesus, 'How much do you love me?' 'This much he answered and he stretched out His arms and died.'"

"Please close your eyes for just a moment. Let's go back 2000 years and think about what it might be like in Jerusalem, during Passover, in the presence of Jesus Christ," Paul started.

"Imagine, your there, sitting on the side of the hill with many others, listening to his stories about life and love and God our Father. He notices you; Jesus looks into your eyes. He knows you and understands your thoughts. Your heart is instantly filled with grace and serenity. Very peaceful and comforting, wouldn't you all agree?"

Lots of yes's were heard throughout the congregation.

"Now let's discuss something not too comfortable, the cross and crucifixion.

"The cross is a symbol of death don't you agree. It's also a symbol of life. How about hate, love? When the guards nailed Jesus to the cross, there was violence then peace. Sin, purity. Defeat then victory. Suffering and sacrifice. There are so many meanings of the Cross."

"Now Imagine that you, back in time, yes you, are on the road to the Crucifixion. You are on the same road as Jesus, Via Dolorosa, you are a spectator, a believer, a follower. Jesus falls, carrying the cross, and falls right next to you."

"Help him up," some shouted.

I got louder, "The guards are all around yelling at you, demanding that you come and lift that cross. They have horses and whips and are intimidating. Are you going to run and hide?"

"Pick up that cross," someone shouts.

"Amen!" shout several more.

I begin to perspire. I feel the change taking place in me. I am no longer Captain Mark Thomas. I am a messenger.

"Are you going to lift that cross? Are you going to help Jesus up? Are you going to risk your personal safety? Remember what I just described, guards are surrounding you, add now that your loved ones are watching and wondering how you are going to react. Jesus is looking right at you, are you going to lift that cross, are you going to lift that cross for Jesus? That's a lot of pressure. Paul here said he would."

I pointed at Paul. The crowd halfheartedly cheered looking at Paul and his masculine stature.

The cameramen moved quickly and focused on Paul. The

audience seemed to all at once, shift in their seats peering at Paul. A few left their seats and headed for the front but were quickly stopped by security and redirected back to their seat.

I look at each face scanning the aisles, one by one and feel their enthusiasm, excitement, and suspense as to what will be said next.

Paul held his arm up with the scar sustained by the guards. Every time Paul looked down at the scar on his arm, he became more and more enthralled and dynamic.

Paul said in a calm monotone voice, "Jesus, I will help carry the cross." The crowd doesn't seem to notice the scar and seemed a bit puzzled by Paul raising his arm, but cheers Paul on for saying he would carry the cross.

Paul told me previously, that at some point in the sermons, he knows that his body is being taken over by a higher power.

"Living the cross-life is demanding but simple. Love God; our neighbors; and care for the needy," added Paul.

"Would you be willing to sustain any injury to help Jesus? He died for you, that's the least you can do for Him. How about our friend, Simon of Cyrene? He carried the cross when Jesus could not anymore. After he lifted the cross, he extended his other hand and lifted Jesus from the ground after He had fallen. By Simon carrying the cross for Jesus is our reminder of the humility of God. God chose Simon for that reason. Here is a man who had done his share, yes, Sy did his share."

I broke in, "Jesus is asking you all right here today; will you help carry my cross? When Jesus took up His cross it was because He was obedient to His Father. He put God's will and His love for us above himself. For by His wounds, you were healed."

Paul chimed in, "He carried our sins in Himself and was

nailed to the cross to pay the penalty for our sins so that we can inherit eternal life. He died for each one of us! He was raised from the dead to give us a new beginning, a new life in Him."

Bursts of "Amen!" filled the Cathedral. Others had worked their way to the alter and had purposedly fallen to the ground, clenching their fists and shaking. Security was no match for the numbers that were heading to the front to be closer.

"Yes, save us Jesus!" others shouted waving their arms high to the heavens.

"Even after the Crucifixion, Simon continued to preach about the events that he himself participated in all the way up to the day he was martyred. Would you, under all these conditions, have helped Jesus then?

"Many of you say yes but that time has passed. We are here, 2000 years later; Jesus again is asking you like it was yesterday; Will you help carry My cross? That cross was and still is a symbol of His love for you and for me. Jesus died for us, the least we can do is take up the cross. You kneel before the crucifix paying the highest honor to our Lord because the cross is inseparable from His sacrifice."

Tears fell from many in attendance as I continued.

"We can't go back in time, but our chance is right here. In our life time."

"He is asking you to help Him, now!"

"There are no soldiers now, no one is forcing you. Will you still bear the cross? In *Luke 9:23, Then He said to them all: 'Whoever wants to be my disciple must deny themselves and take up their cross daily and follow me.'* It means to put aside your selfish desires for others' needs. It's following God's will for our lives. You can do it."

"I will take it!" shouted one from the crowd. "Me too shouts another, me too!"

"Jesus took the time for people. His own plans and agenda didn't take center stage. He gave everything including His life. Open your heart to compassion," Paul said.

"Don't scorn the weight of the cross! There are sick, homeless, people in need, in desperate need looking for Jesus. Will you help him tend to the needy?" In *1 John 3:17 "If anyone sees his brother and fellow believer in need yet closes his heart of compassion against him, how can the love of God live and remain in him?"*

"Do you have time for just a kind word if it's all that's needed? How about a few moments to listen to their concerns? We need to be willing if a situation arises, that we can tend to someone's needs. Even if it means just to take some time to listen. This small act sometimes begins a healing process in that person's life."

I looked over to Paul and see that he is zoned in and ready to add a few things to the sermon. Each time we address an audience, there is no script. We do not have the same sermon ever.

Paul said, "Carry it for a step, two steps, a block, or a mile. Maybe all you can do is wipe away a tear, as Veronica did, do it. Carry that cross every day of your life. There are people in need. There is an unrelenting beauty of the cross."

"Keep your heart of compassion open," I added.

The crowd seemed overly rambunctious now.

"If you get tired, set it down, rest, but pick it up again, don't give up. God is depending on you. God is depending on us up here right now to give you this message. He has a crossed shape plan for your life if you listen to what He is asking of you. His love is unending, His love is strong, His love is unwavering. In return, He asked you to continue and to do the work of Jesus; Talk to God each day. God is easy to talk to. Share with Him your day; your trials and tell Him how grateful you are for all the good things in your life."

There was no one sitting any longer. All were standing extending their arms.

"Ask Him say, 'Father, I want to help carry the cross, tell me what You want me to do.'"

Amens were heard around the church.

"Listen for the reply, and be patient. It may not be right away but you will get an answer. He may ask you to do something that is totally out of your comfort zone. Do it, He will prepare you."

"Amen," the crowd shouted back. Paul walked out in front of the podium. He was sweating profusely. His eyes were closed and his head is tilted back. His arms are extended outward. Some rush to the front to be closer to Paul. They are anticipating a message from him.

All in the audience are now focused on Paul as he yelled out, "Holy Spirit, come to me. Holy Spirit, come to me. Holy Spirit, come to me."

Paul's head was completely saturated. Each time he shook his head when he spoke, water splashed from him like a shower head. Paul raised both arms upward. The audience was mesmerized.

The scar on his arm, the one he received from the guard while he was trying to help with the cross, took on a life of its own. The scar turned a dark red. It was now visible to all. With his arms extended, tiny droplets of blood seep along the edges of his scar.

Cameras zeroed in on Paul's arm and the image was

broadcasted on all the screens. Many in the Cathedral and outside gasp, trying to understand just what Paul was experiencing and the significance of his wound.

Police are holding back people on the outside who are trying to get in to witness first-hand the transfiguration.

Paul hollered out in a strange voice. "Tell us if you are the Christ, 'The Son of God'."

Now speaking in Aramaic, he shouts, "Yes, it is as you say."

Some in the crowd that understand Aramaic, fall to their knees, and pound their chests.

I translate.

"Are you the King of the Jews?" Paul yells in Hebrew.

In Aramaic, he says, "Yes, it is as you say."

Paul begins to thrash back and forth as if he is being scourged. In his exhausted voice he proclaimed, "*Eloi, Eloi, lama sabachthani*?" as he falls to the ground on his knees.

Paul slowly tried to rise from the floor but falls back down due to the exhaustion. It's over. He is fighting now to open his eyes.

With a soft, but resonating scratchy voice I say,

"My God, my God, why have you forsaken me?"

Paul, now with extremely labored breathing, then added in Hebrew, "Father, into your hands I commit my spirit."

I then relayed the message in English.

Weeping was heard throughout the Cathedral.

Two staff members rushed to Paul's side as he begins to convulse. Once they stabilized Paul, they assisted him to a chair near the altar for water and offer him a towel.

Observers were aghast, many holding their hands over their mouths, some holding their hearts, in disbelief at what they just witnessed. Others held an arm in the air with their heads down, rocking back and forth and praying out loud.

Paul sipped the water then rises to a sigh of relief from the audience and returns to his podium near me.

Hundreds of people have moved to the front packing the aisles and, on their knees, and continued praying and listening.

"The heart of Jesus is bigger than you can imagine. He suffered the worst kind of torture that anyone has ever endured; He was nailed to the cross, for you, and you, and you and me. Would you do that, would you put yourself through all that for someone you love, He did!

"He did it because He knew that as God's children, we have committed sins. Sins that would have kept us out of heaven. Jesus did not want that; He wanted us to live in Heaven, eternally, with Him."

"God said to Jesus at the River Jordan, *'You are my beloved Son; with you, I am well pleased.'*

"God wants to say that to each and every one of you. Carry the cross for Him; it may be heavy at times, cumbersome as Paul can relate, but do whatever your heart and body can allow. Push it just a bit further. We can't go back and save Jesus from the Cross, but we can help and eliminate some of the pain He endured, here and now.

"And it is no longer I who live, but it is Christ who lives in me. And the life I now live in the flesh I live by the faith of the Son of God, who loved me and gave himself for me." Galatians 2:20

I moved out from in back of my podium carrying a microphone in one hand and with the other, going through the motion of lifting an imaginary cross. I am joined by Paul.

"Are you okay I asked?" in a closed conversation.

"Fine I guess, not sure what actually happened."

"Symbolically, Paul and I are picking up the cross, we are lifting; we are not afraid of what the guards might think or do to us or for that matter what anyone thinks. We are there to help Jesus, save us. Jesus rose on that glorious Third Day. Will you be there to celebrate the Glory of the Resurrection?" As I spoke, I felt intense heat building up inside of me.

Others came up front and helped us raise the imaginary cross in the air. Many stood with us, hundreds, lifting this imaginary cross.

"Yes, Jesus, yes!" someone shouted from the crowd.

"Will you be with the One who rises on the Third Day in heaven and peeks out through the walls of death and proclaims I am here!"

"Lord, Jesus, yes!"

"Amen." Was the response.

"Will you share your love of Jesus with your family and friends?"

"Amen," they echoed in unison.

Still out of breath, Paul interjected, "Jesus withstood a brutal beating; can you take negative comments from unbelievers without being embarrassed? Will you defend Jesus' love? Don't be afraid, carry that cross, reach in if you have to when someone is stumbling, reach in to grab that cross, and don't be afraid of the whips, reach in until that cross is no longer an obstacle."

The crowd applauded in agreement.

I cut Paul off and shouted, "Someday, when your cross is falling, and you cannot bear the weight anymore, someone will reach in to help you. When you look at the cross think of God's love and forgiveness for you, and the sacrifice that Jesus has made for us, and, perhaps every now and then think about Sy,

Simon of Cyrene who was there to help Jesus carry the cross. Simon carried that cross for Jesus; others there on that final day helped Simon also. Do not be afraid to help fulfill the mission that Jesus started. Be kind and caring. Live your life through the way of the cross.

"The cross is something else, it's a symbol of life, a symbol of honor and a symbol of eternal victory."

Tears of joy, fear, and adoration engulfed the auditorium. People's hands lifted in the air. The message had been delivered.

When we finished speaking, we were both drenched, soaked and completely depleted. There was no combat mission that would compare to the physical energy that both of us had used during the sermon. People knew that we were genuine. They heard it and felt it. Nothing in our message was scripted. We went out and God spoke through us.

As we accepted handshakes from those around and praise for doing God's work, a well-dressed man approached and handed Paul an envelope with a gold seal. He thanked the gentleman and handed the envelope to Gabe who was standing behind us. Gabe opened the ornate envelope. Gabe leaned forward between Paul and me and whispered with a smile,

"You boys have just been invited to the Vatican."

"Great Gabe..."

Silence... I turn to see what I was feeling.

A somber look now appeared across Gabe's face.

"What...what is it? What's wrong?" noticing that Gabe now is acting completely out of character and not his usual upbeat self.

With his head down, staring at the letter, he looks back up and says, "It goes on to say 'and bring the Veil.' No one knows about the Veil," Gabe says.

The choir in the background began to softly sing the hymn, 'Were You There when they crucified my Lord?'

When we left, the church bells rang, and rang and rang.

ACKNOWLEDGMENTS

First, to my mother and father who brought me into this world but had to leave suddenly leaving me with my older sisters and brother, Gerry, Joanne, Delores, and Bob. They each had their own unique style that has guided me in good times and bad in the absence of my parents. At times when I questioned Delores, her reply was, “What, are you writing a book?” Yes, I am now.

I was blessed with my three kids, Michael, Brian, and Tracey who taught me selflessness. Hence, my seven grandchildren, Klohie, Meladie, Alex, Rowan, Emily, Madeline, and Lucy. I hope my book plants a seed in their hearts to one day flourish knowing they are the children of Almighty God.

To my Bible study group, Dwight, Jeff, and Guy, who opened my eyes to understand just what Christianity is.

To all I crossed paths with in life; my many friends, extended family, co-workers, teammates, acquaintances and others, each one of you has left a memory, on my mind, heart, and soul.

To my friend and baseball buddy, editor and mentor, Frank Amoroso. You taught me humility and perseverance. You have guided me on the field and off, teaching me that writing is not only from your mind, but also from your heart.

Lastly, but most importantly I would like to thank my wife, Monta. She has always supported my endeavors and has walked with me side by side.

Made in the USA
Middletown, DE
02 February 2024

48976800R10133